GRAVE APOLOGIES

by

J.W. Mets

DORRANCE
PUBLISHING CO
EST. 1920
PITTSBURGH, PENNSYLVANIA 15235

Dorrance Publishing Co
585 Alpha Drive
Pittsburgh, PA 15238
Visit our website at www.dorrancebookstore.com

ISBN: 979-8-88729-149-9
eISBN: 979-8-88729-649-4

Chapter One: A Later Night

Smoke from a barely lit cigarette wisped around in the air like a lost spirit only visible through the scattered moonlight that snaked in through the window curtains. A man laid in bed as he held his cigarette loosely with his lips. Smoke slipped out through his nose as a woman sat up next to him in the bed, the blanket loosely covering her naked body.

"Well, you certainly know how to show a girl one more good night," the girl said in a playful manner, the moonlight caressing her features as she looked at the man.

"Well, I'd be pretty shit at my job if I didn't, now, wouldn't I?" the guy said as he got out of bed. The smoke from his cigarette followed him closely. The woman stood behind him, laying gentle kisses on his neck before he turned around. "Besides, a beautiful soul such as you deserves a nice night every now and then, especially in a place like this."

The woman smiled and spun around in the blanket before leaning against the air.

"You help make the afterlife so much more pleasing, Hyde baby." The woman grabbed her dress off the floor as Hyde put on his black shirt and trench coat.

"And you make life worth dying for, Gracie baby." Hyde put his hat on with a bow before leaving Gracie alone in the room.

As Hyde walked through the dim halls of the hotel, he pulled a new cigarette out of the pack and lit it with a snap of his fingers. Hyde walked down the stairs into the main room of the hotel, and the sound of a jazz piano could be heard from the bar. "A drink couldn't hurt." Hyde smiled under the brim of his hat and walks into the bar. Cigar and cigarette smoke filled the room, and on the brightly lit stage a jazz band was performing some song about an ugly girl with pretty eyes. Hyde took a seat at the bar and ordered a double shot of whiskey neat before turning his attention to the band.

The whole bar was full of people enjoying the afterlife as well as people just enjoying a day off from work. This was Hyde's life; both the dead and the living came to him with problems relating to the supernatural.

"Your whiskey, sir." The bartender slid the tumbler into Hyde's hand.

"Much appreciated, boss." Hyde pointed at the bartender before taking a sip of the whiskey. As he did this, he felt a tap on his shoulder. As Hyde turned around, he saw a meek little man standing behind him, nervously holding his hand in his hands. "Can I help you?" Hyde said as he turned around to fully face the man.

"A-are you Hyde Paranormal PI?" the guy spoke softly, his voice almost drowned out by the dramatic solo of the band's saxophone player. Hyde nodded and took another sip of his whiskey.

"Yeah, that's me. Why? You got a problem with something spooky?" Hyde chuckled to himself as the man sat next to him.

"I think my wife is trying to kill me."

Hyde put the glass down and nodded. "Why's that my problem?"

The man sighed and ordered a seltzer water before telling Hyde his problem. "Because she's been dead for a few days now. I know I might not look it, but I work closely with the mob and more specifically the mob's money. I handle all inner and outer expenses and the like." The guy took a shaky drink of his seltzer before continuing. "Well, things started to take a bad turn lately, and I couldn't keep up, so I did what no mobster should ever do and stepped back. I thought I'd be okay, but last week I came home from my new job and found my wife's head on her pillow." The man began to quietly cry. Hyde put a hand on the guy's shoulder.

"No more needed. I'll take the case and help put your wife to rest."

The man smiled and wiped his tears. "Thank you, mister. Here's my address. Please meet me there tomorrow afternoon." Hyde nodded and the guy left him to his drink and music.

The bartender walked over to Hyde as he wiped down a whiskey tumbler. "Back to back clients today, Hyde. Surely you can pay off your tab now?" The bartender raised his eyebrow toward Hyde as he stood from his seat.

"Ah, you'd think so, Jack, but sadly no." Hyde smiled and put his hat on. "Tell the wife I said hi," Hyde said as he left the bar and walked outside the hotel. It was a cold night and the wind was sharp and cut to the bone. Hyde fixed his jacket and looked at the sign on the hotel.

"See ya, AfterLife. Such a fitting name." Hyde chuckled at his thought and began to walk to his car. The wind pulled at his jacket playfully before he got to his car. "Hey Rosey, sorry I took so long to get back to ya. You're probably freezing."

A woman appeared by the passenger side door with a long cigarette holder held between her fingers. She smelled of smoke and sweet perfume.

"You leave me in this cold for that long again and I will haunt you instead of this car. Got it, Hyde?"

Hyde opened the driver side door and took his hat off as he got inside. "Hey now, doll, no reason for the hostility. You know I don't do it on purpose." Hyde started the car as Rosey sat next to him and sighed.

"So where to now?" Rosey looked at her face in a small pocket mirror she kept on her at all times as Hyde began to drive through the city streets.

"We gots ourselves a job for tomorrow. I'm just doin' some surveillance of the area. With it bein' mob territory, I don't need you or me g'tting' filled with lead, and by you I mean the car."

"Since when do you work with mobsters? I thought they gave you a headache?"

Hyde fixed his grip on the wheel as he put a cigarette to his lips. "Normally they do, but the guy who gave us the job wants us to help put his wife to rest." Hyde looked out the window at the dock they were passing,

"Aww, I loves me a good romance." Rosey put her hands over her heart. "If I was breathin', I think my heart would be all a-fuckin' flutter."

Hyde nodded in silence as he took a drag from his cigarette before letting out a slow sigh.

"Yeah, romance is nice, if you believe in that shit." Hyde parked the car by a warehouse and grabbed his hat before getting out of the car.

Rosey leaned out the window and looked his way. "Don't you leave me here for another two fuckin' hours. Got it, sweetie?"

Hyde held his hand up to Rosey as he walked down the dock. Unease washed over Hyde like a wave crashing into the side of the dock and he gripped his pistol tightly.

"This place is so full of death and unsettled anger it makes me sick," Hyde thought to himself as he turned a corner to see two mobsters talking. Quickly Hyde hid behind a nearby oil drum and began to eavesdrop on the conversation.

"Did ya hear what the boss had that new kid do?"

"Yeah, brutal how he did it, too. I didn't think the little shit could do it."

"Wonder what he did with the body afterwards."

"I heard the sick fuck still has it with him." The mobsters continued talking for a few minutes before someone else came and collected them, leaving Hyde with a solid idea as to how to handle the job. Rosey stood outside the car waiting for Hyde, and eventually she saw him coming back to the car lost in thought.

"Well, did you find anything out? Or did we waste our time?"

"No, I just found out how deep we really are in this shit. Get in the car. We're heading home."

On the drive back, Hyde filled Rosey in on everything he had found out. Her face showed the disgust she was feeling without her needing to say anything. Hyde and Rosey got out of the car and walked into the apartment he lived in. Once there, Hyde started thinking about what he got himself into.

"So what're you thinking?" Rosey stood by the window, looking out at the city that had killed her so long ago.

Hyde put his hands together and sighed. "What we always do: put a spirit to rest." Hyde leaned back on his loveseat and put his hat over his face. "Wake me in the morin', okay, doll? Thanks."

Rosey looked at Hyde as she stood by the window; she felt a slight smile form on her face before she looked back out the window.

In the morning Hyde was woken up by a cold yet gentle touch on his arm followed by Rosey's gentle voice.

"Hey, wake up. We got a job to do." Rosey took Hyde's hat off his face and handed him a cigarette. "Here, I know these always wake you up."

Hyde put the cigarette between his lips and sat up.

"Thanks, Rosey, I owe you." Hyde stood up and rubbed his shoulder. The sunlight crept in through the blinds, illuminating the mess that his apartment had become. Rosey tossed Hyde his hat and walked to the door.

"When was the last time you had a real breakfast and not just a cigarette and sometimes black coffee?"

Hyde grabbed his jacket as he thought of an answer. "Probably a year before I started helping spirits." Hyde closed and locked the door and started walking to the car; as he did, he couldn't help but think about his life before he started doing what he does, when he was a normal investigator solving normal crimes. "Oh how times have changed," Hyde thought to himself as he opened the driver side door.

Hyde looked at the address one last time before he began the drive. Rosey looked out the window at the city as it passed her by.

"Why do you do it, Hyde?"

"Do what?" Hyde looked over at Rosey from the corner of his eye as she fixed her hair in the mirror.

"Save spirits. I mean, you aren't some priest and it's not like you get anything from this." Rosey looked at Hyde as he drove. "No normal breather would do something like this, yet here you are, driving a haunted car to go and put some schmuck's wife to rest."

Hyde took a long slow drag of his cigarette before letting the smoke leave his lungs.

"I couldn't tell ya, Rose. I just do it to do it, I suppose." Hyde parked the car outside the house and grabbed his hat off the dashboard. "I shouldn't be too long."

"Don't get killed!" Rosey yelled at Hyde as he got out of the car and walked up to the front door.

Hyde felt a knot form in his stomach as he walked up to the door, and it only got worse when he knocked on it. It didn't take long before the man from yesterday had opened the door for Hyde.

"You actually came. Oh thank god." The man stepped back, letting Hyde inside his home. "So how does this work? Is there a prayer involved or…" The man stopped as Hyde pulled a revolver out from it's holster.

"I'll need you to leave."

The man laughed nervously. "I did tell you she's already dead. I don't think a pistol is necessary, sir."

Hyde sighed and unloaded one of his bullets. "These are specially made for pissed-off spirits. There's purified salt mixed in with the metal and gunpowder in the bullet; it weakens the spirit, making them easier to handle. Now, please leave. It's going to get very dangerous in here." Hyde chuckled as he reloaded the bullet. "And I can't have you dying on me before you pay me."

The man nodded and quickly left his home. Once the door closed, Hyde put his hat on a little snugger and began walking around the old home.

Every step was followed by creaking wood planks, and the sound of the whistling through all the hidden cracks of the home would've made any sane person want to leave; fortunately Hyde wasn't the most sane person in the world.

The man stood outside, impatiently pacing back and forth waiting for Hyde to finish. Rosey saw him and decided to help take his mind off the job.

"Hey, mister," Rosey said as she got out of the car and walked over to the man. "What's your name?"

The man looked at Rosey as she walked up to him and leaned against the railing on the stairway.

"Oh, it's Clark, miss, and yours?" The man stopped pacing, but still seemed worried.

"It's Rosey. Nice to meet ya, Clark." Rosey held her hand out to Clark and gave him her best smile. "You don't need to worry. Hyde does this almost every day." A pistol shot could be heard from inside as Rosey finished her sentence.

"I-is that normal?" Clark put a cigarette in his mouth and tried to light a match, but his nerves were making his hands too shaky. Rosey lit his cigarette with her lighter and nodded.

"Hyde does things in a rather unconventional method, but he always gets the job done."

Hyde pushed the table that had been thrown at him off with a grunt and aimed his gun at the monstrous spirit as it wailed like a banshee.

"Damn, doll, you are one ugly bitch." Hyde chuckled and spit some blood out as the spirit yelled and charged at him. Hyde went to shoot but when he pulled the trigger, all he heard was the depressing click of an empty revolver. "Shit." The spirit grabbed Hyde and slammed him into a wall before throwing him down a set of stairs.

"I WON'T BE PUT TO REST!"

Hyde got on his hands and knees as he coughed up more blood before getting to his feet.

"Well, that just won't work because your husband doesn't want you killing him." Hyde began to reload his pistol as the spirit charged at him from the top of the stairs.

"ALL HIS FAULT!" The spirit went to tackle Hyde, but as she did, he put the barrel right between her eyes and pulled the trigger. The spirit cried out and reeled back in pain; as she did that, Hyde put his left hand on her chest. When he did, the spirit's monstrous form faded away, leaving the spirit's true form. She looked at Hyde as he held his ribs and coughed up some more blood.

"Oh heavens, please let me help you."

Hyde held up his hand as he put his pistol in the holster. "You don't have much time. Save it for your husband, I'll go get him."

"Yes, please do."

Hyde walked outside and saw Rosey and Clark talking. "Job's done."

Clark turned around and gasped, seeing Hyde in the state he was in. "Christ, are you—"

Hyde cut Clark off. "Go say your good-byes. She doesn't have long." Clark nodded and quickly ran inside, leaving Hyde and Rosey alone.

"Take it I'm driving?" Rosey laughed as she put a hand on Hyde's shoulder.

Clark came outside soon after with tear-stained cheeks and red eyes. "Thank you so much, Hyde." Clark's voice was broken and raspy from crying, and he took shaky breaths between his sentences. "Thank you so much for giving me one last laugh with my beloved." Clark handed Hyde an envelope. "I know we didn't discuss a price, but that moment was worth everything in that envelope." Clark smiled as tears rolled down his eyes before he walked back inside. Hyde put the envelope in his jacket and grunted in pain as he walked down the stairs.

"I need a drink," Hyde said as he leaned against the car.

"The AfterLife I'm guessing, then." Rosey laughed as she got in the driver seat. "Try not to get too much blood on my seats, got it?"

Hyde nodded. "Yeah, yeah, I got it." Hyde put his hat over his face and closed his eyes. As sleep washed over him like a gentle blanket, he saw a beautiful woman with dark hair and gorgeous red lips. The woman smiled and put her hands on Hyde's cheeks and whispered, "Don't give up on us, baby."

Hyde woke up as Rosey parked the car outside the AfterLife.

"Hey, we're here." Hyde took his hat off his face and sat up slowly. "You know, you'd like it in there. Both breathers and spirits live together and no one's the wiser. The booze ain't the best, but the band ain't bad." Hyde smiled as he opened the door.

"I'll pass for now, but thanks for the offer." Rosey faded away, leaving Hyde alone with his wounds. Hyde walked into the AfterLife and heard the smooth music the band was playing in the bar. The smell of the cheap perfumes and strong cigars filled his nose. Hyde walked up to the front desk and rang the desk bell; it broke the silence with a slightly out-of-tune ding.

"I'll be right there." A voice followed the ding from the back room and soon a young well-dressed man walked out of the back room and gasped as he saw Hyde. "Sir, are you okay? You should be in a hospital." Hyde shook his head and adjusted his hat.

"No need. Just give me the key to room sixteen."

The man hesitantly gave Hyde the key and watched as he walked over to the stairs. Hyde stumbled through the hallway until he got to room sixteen. With a shaky hand, he unlocked the door and walked inside. As the door closed behind him, he dropped to one knee with a pained grunt. Hyde held his ribs as he heard a familiar voice.

"Rough night, Hyde baby?" Gracie said as she walked up to Hyde and carefully took his hat off. Hyde nodded and carefully got onto the dingy bed, the rusted springs creaking loudly.

"Do you still have that bottle up here, babe, or did we drink it all?" Gracie nodded and handed Hyde a bottle of whiskey. The amber-colored liquor sloshed around in the bottle as Hyde pressed the head of it to his lips and took a long drink. The whiskey burned on the way down but gave Hyde something else to think about other than the pain in his ribs. Gracie rubbed Hyde's shoulders. Her cold fingertips snaked around Hyde's body as she leaned in closely and kissed the back of his neck.

"I've missed your warmth, Hyde."

Hyde gently put a hand on one of Gracie's as he put the bottle of whiskey on the floor.

"And I've been thinking about your cold touch all day." Hyde turned around and placed a kiss on Gracie's cold pink lips.

Rosey stood outside the car looking at the AfterLife's sign, her cigarette casting a dim orange glow on her pale lips.

"Fuckin' idiot makin me worry about him." Rosey dropped the butt of her cigarette and stomped it flat. "Get it together, Rosey. He ain't worth your worry," Rosey thought to herself as she opened the passenger side door and checked her seat. "At least he kept his blood off my seats."

Hyde laid in bed with his left hand on his ribs, a dim glow creeping out from under his palm. Gracie looked over at Hyde as she rubbed his chest.

"You're unlike any breather I've come across, both when I was alive and now that I'm dead."

Hyde looked down at Gracie and chuckled in his throat. "What makes you say that, darlin'?"

Gracie sat up and put Hyde's hat on her head and smiled. "Well, you seem to really care about us spirits, and it's nice to feel cared for."

Hyde moved his hand and sighed as he sat up. "Yeah." Hyde grabbed his shirt and took his hat off Gracie's head. "Take care of yourself, darlin'." Gracie looked over at Hyde as he put his jacket on.

"Be safe out there. Everyone has a limit, supernatural or not." Gracie smiled as she faded away, leaving Hyde alone in the room.

"Yeah, will do." Hyde left the room and walked back to the front desk. As he walked through the hallway, he heard some of the other guests in the AfterLife. Some laughed, some cried, but most, most argued. The AfterLife was one hell of a place for both living and dead guests. Hyde got to the front desk and tossed the key onto the counter before leaving the hotel.

Hyde walked outside, and as he did he was stopped by two guys in rather expensive-looking suits.

"Can I help you two?" Hyde said as he placed a cigarette between his lips. One of the guys placed a hand on Hyde's shoulder.

"We need you to come with us," the other guy said in a stern, choked-up voice. The guy grabbing Hyde's shoulder tightened his grip and smiled.

Hyde looked him in the eyes; they were small and dark, his face was rough and slightly bruised with cauliflower ears set on each side of his head.

"And if I don't? What happens then?"

The other guy chuckled and showed Hyde his pistol. "Let's not make this ugly, shall we?"

Hyde was about to hit the guy but as his fist tightened he heard Rosey's voice.

"What have I told you about leaving me out here, asshole!" Rosey walked over to Hyde and the other two guys and looked at them. "Are you two schmucks the reason I'm not home yet?" Rosey wasted no time and slapped the man who threatened to shoot Hyde, then looked at the one holding his shoulder. "And what're you doing?" Hyde stopped Rosey by grabbing her wrist as she went to slap the guy.

"All right, all right, thank you, gentlemen, for the offer, but I'm afraid if you want to talk to me you'll have to call my office." Hyde handed the guy who got slapped a card with a number on it.

"Have a nice night, gentlemen." Hyde turned around and started walking with Rosey while she chewed him out.

Chapter Two: Worth It

Rosey stayed mostly quiet during the car ride back to the apartment, but Hyde could feel her stabbing him with her glare. Rosey finally broke the silence as she turned to face Hyde. "So who were those goons anyway?"

Hyde let one hand slip from the wheel and rested it on the door as he watched the road.

"Not sure. Probably just two assholes trying to give me a hard time. I was on the force a few years back."

Hyde and Rosey got out of the car and started walking to the apartment. When they got inside, Hyde walked over to the kitchen and poured himself a double of whiskey.

"You want anything, Rosey?" Hyde said as he swirled his glass.

"No, I'll be okay." Rosey opened the window before lighting her cigarette. Hyde leaned against the kitchen doorway and took a sip of his whiskey.

"What's troubling you, darlin'?" Hyde looked Rosey up and down. Her short blonde hair matched her pale skin perfectly, and she almost seemed alive in the moonlight, her cigarette casting that same dim glow as she inhaled the smoke before letting it creep out from her pale pink lips.

"This city. It's built on murder and crime, yet no one seems to mind it." Hyde walked up to Rosey as she looked out the window. "I died in that car, Hyde, yet they never found the bastard who took my life." Rosey put the cigarette to her lips with a calm hand, yet she took a shaky drag from it.

"You've never talked to me about your death. Why do it now?" Hyde leaned against the wall looking upon his messy apartment, the only light coming from a lamp on his desk and the gentle stream of moonlight that passed through Rosey's body.

"I remember when I woke up in that car, I was in the back seat." Rosey flicked the butt of her cigarette out the window and watched as it faded away before even touching the ground. "I didn't even realize I was dead until I heard two guys talking about my body, and how the cops couldn't find any evidence to make a clean case." Rosey turned and looked at Hyde as he sipped his whiskey. "Then you come along and buy that shitty car off some auction, and now I'm playing cops and robbers with some idiot I know barely anything about."

Hyde turned and looked down at Rosey, placing a gentle hand on her cheek to carefully wipe away the single tear she let slip out.

"Cut the waterworks. There's no reason to be crying right now, Rose." Hyde pulled his hand away slowly and tucked it in his pocket as he walked toward his desk. "I told you when we first met that I'd avenge you, didn't I?"

Rosey looked at Hyde with surprise in her eyes as he put his glass down. "You remembered?"

"Of course I did. What kind of man would I be if I broke a promise I made to a lady in need?" Hyde smiled before yawning into the back of his hand. "I'm thinkin' that a good night's sleep in my bed is what I need right now." Hyde put his hat on his desk and winked toward Rosey before walking back to his room.

Rosey blushed and looked out the window at the city that had killed her so long ago.

Hyde unbuttoned his shirt and let it drop to the floor before he crawled into bed. A deep sleep soon took hold of him and soon Hyde dreamt of that woman once again. She wore a short red dress that hugged her hips; her dark hair covered her eyes, yet her lips drew all of Hyde's attention.

The woman leaned in close to Hyde and he could smell her perfume; it was faint but he could make out oranges and vanilla. The woman's hands were soft and felt at home on Hyde's chest.

"Be safe for me, baby. I hate seeing you get hurt." Hyde went to hold the woman, but as his hands touched her sides, she faded away, leaving Hyde alone with the scent of her perfume still hanging around his nose. He felt a single tear fall from his eye, yet he couldn't understand why.

In the morning Hyde was woken up by the screaming of his desk phone. He dragged himself out of bed and stumbled to his desk.

"Hello." Hyde's voice was rough and gravelly, yet the voice coming from the phone felt like velvet in his ears.

"Hello, is this Hyde, the um…paranormal investigator?"

Hyde cleared his throat and stood up straight as he held the phone. "Yeah, this is. What can I do for you today, ma'am?" Hyde grabbed his notepad and a pen.

"Well, I'd rather not speak of it over the phone. Perhaps you could meet me at Charity?"

Hyde stood, puzzled. "That restaurant downtown?"

"Yes, please. If you could meet me there this afternoon, I'd be delighted."

"Will do, ma'am., Hyde said before the woman hung up her end of the line.

Hyde rubbed his head and looked at the window where he and Rosey talked last night. The light from the sun stabbed through the blinds, dust daintially floated in the beams of sunlight. Hyde walked back to his room and got dressed for the day, visions of that woman still plagued his mind.

"Nothing some booze can't fix," Hyde mumbled under his breath as he grabbed his jacket off its hanger. Rosey met Hyde by the kitchen and watched as he grabbed the almost-empty whiskey bottle.

"Rough night, I'm guessing?" Rosey said as Hyde poured himself a single shot.

"Wasn't the best, but we got a job today." Hyde took the shot before continuing his sentence. "We're meeting the client at Charity." Rosey's eyes widened with a strange mix of shock and confusion.

"Charity, as in that fancy-ass restaurant with the dancers? That Charity?"

Hyde nodded as Rosey leaned against the counter. "Yeah, that's the place." Hyde grabbed his hat off his desk and placed it on his head before opening the door to the apartment.

Rosey walked next to Hyde and looked up at him, his sleepless eyes and rough intimidating gaze focused ahead of him. His eyes never wandered like most people's. Rosey's eyes traced the outline of Hyde's face until they had left the apartment building where she snapped herself out of the trance she was in. Hyde got in the driver's seat and waited for Rosey.

"So, what's the job entail?" Rosey said as she placed a cigarette loosely between her lips.

"Not sure. She wouldn't tell me anything over the phone, not even her name." Hyde looked over at Rosey as she tried to light her cigarette. After a few seconds of trying to spark her lighter Hyde snapped his fingers and lit her cigarette for her. Rosey's cheek blushed a faint pink color as she pulled the cigarette out of her mouth.

"Asshole, I almost had it." Hyde chuckled as he started the car and began to drive off.

"Where we goin'?" Rosey said before putting the cigarette back in her mouth.

"Figured I'd head over to Charity now and get a scope of the place before I actually sit down in it." Hyde's eyes locked on the road as Rosey's darted from building to building.

"I used to perform downtown," Rosey said as she looked at her burning cigarette in between her fingers, the smoke slowly snaking off the dim flame. "I was a singer, you know?" Rosey said with a sigh as she placed the cigarette between her lips once again.

"Did you like singin'?"

"Loved it. I always had butterflies in my stomach and chest right before the show, but once I stepped out in front of that crowd." Rosey stopped and smiled for a brief moment. "It was beautiful."

Hyde nodded and pulled into the Charity parking lot.

"You comin' in with me?" Hyde looked over at Rosey as she stared out the window at the building. "Rosey," Hyde said in a more stern tone, which startled her out of her trance.

"Huh? Oh, um…n-no, I'll wait out here." Rosey gave Hyde a soft smile before turning back to the window. Hyde shrugged and closed the car door, leaving Rosey alone.

Hyde made his way around the large building. Muffled music could be heard from the otherside of the brick walls. As he walked around the building, he began to hear voices coming from around the corner.

"Do you even believe in all this supernatural bullshit?" said one of the voices. "I mean, come on, ghosts aren't real. Just listen to yourself."

"I'm telling you, that guy's bad fucking news. He threw the boss against a wall without even touching him, and now boss has these bruises all over his neck like someone was choking him." The second voice spoke quickly and with a panicked tone.

Hyde nodded and began walking back to the car. As he did he felt something watching him from over his shoulder. Quickly Hyde turned around with his pistol drawn, but when he did there was no one behind him. Just an empty alleyway filled with trash, rats, and smoke that billowed up from loose manhole covers. Hyde put his pistol away and placed a hand over his heart as he let out a shaky breath.

Hyde made it back to the car and quickly sat in the driver's seat. Rosey appeared in the passenger's seat and looked over at him.

"What happened?" Rosey looked at Hyde's face. His eyes shook in their socket,s but his face still remained calm and collected.

"I've got a bad feeling about this job." Hyde put his hand on the wheel as he started the car.

They had a few hours before the client would be at Charity, so Hyde decided to do some more investigating. Rosey looked at Hyde as he drove. His lips barely held onto his cigarette and the worry that was in his eyes had been replaced by their normal determined yet dead stare. Rosey reached out and gently touched Hyde's arm.

"Hey, you know you can talk to me, right? I mean, we are partners in this job, aren't we?" Rosey smiled at Hyde, but he didn't return the affection; he never did.

"Yeah, we are." Hyde pulled into a nearby warehouse yard. As he parked Rosey grabbed his sleeve and looked him in the eyes.

"I want to come this time." Rosey grabbed the spare pistol Hyde kept in the glove box and held it with both hands as she waited for Hyde's answer.

"Okay, let's do this," Hyde said as he opened his door. He and Rosey got out of the car and looked around.

"So what're we looking for, Mr. Detective?" Rosey said as she walked next to Hyde.

"Signs of a supernatural presence." Hyde put his hands in the pockets of his jacket as the smoke from his cigarette swirled passed his head.

"Like other spirits?" Rosey said with a hint of confusion in her voice.

"Not quite. More like left behind traces of magic similar to what I use to put evil spirits to rest."

Rosey nodded as she held her pistol tighter.

As they walked through the spaces between each warehouse, the wind danced around them, playing with their looser clothes as it moved around them. Hyde stopped and pulled his left hand out of his pocket and looked at his palm.

"Something's close." Hyde looked around at the warehouses. Finally his eyes locked on a dirty, rust-covered warehouse. "Over there."

Rosey followed Hyde as he moved toward the rundown building. As they got closer to the door, the air grew more and more stale and hung more heavily around them. Hyde put his hand on the door before entering. Once his palm touched the rust-covered door, he felt a sinister wave of emotion rush into him.

Hyde pulled his hand off the door calmly before pushing the door open with his shoulder, drawing his pistol as he entered. Rosey followed behind him closely.

"Yuck! It smells like rotten meat." Rosey covered her mouth and nose as she gagged. The air within the warehouse was heavy and was filled with negative emotions. Hyde's left hand began to burn slightly as he looked around. His investigation was interrupted as a thin man suddenly appeared in front of him and sent Hyde flying back a few feet with a strike from his palm. Rosey took aim and shot at the guy, but he managed to dodge the bullets. The man laughed loudly as he moved around Rosey's shots. Hyde coughed as he got up after being attacked.

"Pretty shitty move, attacking someone out of the blue like that, don't ya think?" Hyde dusted himself off and fixed his hat as the man bowed in front of him and Rosey.

"My utmost apologies, sir. I just hate noisy people."

Hyde looked at the man that attacked him; he had a slender figure and snow-white hair. The man wore a dark red vest with a white undershirt and gloves to match, and his black dress pants were adorned with two silver chains that hung slightly below his pockets. Finally a black eyepatch covered his right eye. Hyde's hand burned more as he looked at the man.

"Consider your apologie not fucking excepted, asshole." Hyde drew his gun and fired a few shots at the man; however, none hit their mark as the man danced between the bullets.

"I'd love to stay and chat, but I have a very important meeting to attend." The man bowed once again before disappearing in a cloud of smoke.

Rosey walked over to Hyde as he reloaded his gun. "Well, that was definitely something I've never seen before." Rosey sighed as Hyde put his gun back in the holster.

"Yeah, same here. I didn't know it was possible to dodge bullets." Hyde reached in his inner jacket pocket and pulled out a silver pocket watch. "We should leave. I don't feel like being late."

Rosey nodded and followed Hyde out of the warehouse. She looked around at the many warehouses as she thought about what her and Hyde were doing.

Hyde and Rosey got back to the car and started driving back to Charity. As they did Hyde continued to try and piece together the puzzle that was just dropped into his lap. Eventually they made it back to Charity and as Hyde parked the car. Rosey faded away making it pretty clear Hyde was doing this alone.

Hyde walked into the restaurant and looked around. Large chandeliers hung from the ceiling as people in expensive suits and dresses enjoyed even more expensive food and wine. Soft music played from the center of the restaurant that could've easily put Hyde to sleep if he wasn't so focused. Hyde looked around some more before a man with a tray stopped him.

"Are you the, um, investigator?" The man seemed disgusted to even talk to Hyde, let alone be seen with him.

"Yeah, that's me. I'm here to meet with a client." Hyde's tone had a mix of annoyance and hatred in it as he spoke to the waiter.

"Please follow me." The waiter spoke in a snobby tone and walked with his head held way too high for Hyde's liking. The waiter took Hyde to a table in the far back of the restaurant. Sitting there was a woman with a large black hat that covered her face with the long brim, a single white feather stuck to the side of it. Hyde sat across from the woman and as he did he fixed his hat to uncover his eyes.

"It's nice to finally meet you, Mr. Hyde," the woman said in that same velvety smooth voice she had over the phone. "My name's Lynn. Tina Lynn, but I'm not too fond of my first name, so I'd appreciate you just call me Lynn." Lynn held her hand out gently to Hyde. A black lace glove covered her hand and forearm.

Hyde shook her hand and cleared his throat before speaking. "Nice to meet you, Lynn. Now then, what's troubling you."

Lynn took her hand back and gently adjusted her hat so Hyde could see her face. Her skin was a beautiful porcelain white, and dark lipstick sucked in Hyde's attention. Her eyes were also like beautiful amber daggers staring directly into Hyde's soul.

"Ah yes, well, I believe someone is trying to kill me, Mr. Hyde." Lynn calmly brought her glass of red wine to her lips and smiled as she took a sip.

"I think you should go to the normal cops with a problem like that." Hyde was about to stand up, but Lynn stopped him.

"I believe they're using my late husband's ghost to kill me, Mr. Hyde." Lynn looked at Hyde as he sat back down in his seat. "You see, my husband loved to gamble; however, he was never any good and two weeks ago he lost a gamble to a rather odd gentleman, and well, now I'm a lone widow." Lynn placed her fingers on the stem of her wine glass as she continued speaking. "Now I can hardly sleep at night without being plagued by these ghastly night terrors, and well." Lynn tilted her head exposing her bruised neck. "The attacks from my husband aren't helping either." Lynn sipped her wine as Hyde reached into his jacket and pulled out a notepad and pencil.

"This man that your husband lost to, can you describe him to me, please?" Hyde looked up from his notepad as Lynn smelled her wine.

"Ah, yes, of course. He was a rather tall and slender gentleman." Lynn paused and thought a bit before continuing, "Ah, yes, and he dressed in a rather strange manner."

"Strange as in how?" Hyde tapped the lead of his pencil on the notepad, waiting for Lynn's answer.

"He wore a red vest and a white undershirt with the sleeves rolled up slightly, and he had odd silver chains adorning his pants." Visions of the man from earlier flooded Hyde's mind as Lynn continued speaking. "His hair was also snow-white, and the strangest part of his attire was the black eyepatch that covered his right eye." Lynn blushed in embarrassment. "I do apologize, but that's all I remember of him, but please tell me you'll help me this man is turning my dear husband into a monster of a man." Lynn touched her neck gently. "He'd never hurt me. He loved me too much. Don't you understand?"

Hyde nodded and stood up from his seat. "I'll save your husband and stop this man from hurting you any further."

Lynn smiled and quickly stood up, "Oh, thank you so much, Mr.Hyde. You don't understand how much this means to me." Lynn walked up to Hyde and reached her hand in between her breasts before pulling out a small piece of paper. She then placed a kiss on the paper before handing it to Hyde. "My number. Please call me when you finish or if you need any more information." Lynn winked quickly before walking away from Hyde and disappearing into the crowd of people.

Hyde put the paper in his inner jacket pocket and left the restaurant. As he walked to his car he saw Rosey leaning against the front of the car having a cigarette.

"Sorry for just disappearing on you earlier. I was just a little shaken up, that's all."

Hyde stood next to Rosey and put a cigarette between his lips. "It's fine." Hyde sighed as he thought about the shit he just stepped into. As he stood there his cigarette unlit he just wondered if this was going to be worth it.

Rosey touched Hyde's arm and snapped him out of his trance. "What happened in there? I haven't seen you this shaken in a long time, Hyde."

Hyde sighed before looking at Rosey. "Care to talk over a drink? I need to clear my head."

Rosey nodded and opened the passenger side door as Hyde walked over to the driver side.

"The AfterLife?" Rosey said as she adjusted herself in her seat.

"Sounds like a plan." Hyde put his hat on the dash before starting the car and driving off.

The whole ride to AfterLife, Hyde couldn't stop thinking about that guy at the warehouse. They eventually made it to AfterLife and Rosey was the first one out of the car. Hyde followed her lead as they walked to the entrance. Rosey walked in ahead of Hyde and heard the jazz band playing in the bar. The song reminded her of her days on the stage and she couldn't help but smile slightly.

Hyde walked up behind Rosey and beckoned her to follow him into the bar. As they walked into the room, the dim lights and smell of cigarettes and cigars filled Rosey with a sense of nostalgia and happiness.

"This isn't as bad as I thought it would be." Rosey sat next to Hyde at the bar as he ordered his usual drink of choice before looking at Rosey. Her gaze was fixated on the band as they played a smooth somber instrumental. Hyde smiled a little before turning back to his drink.

"You should go up and sing. I'm sure the people in here would love a new sound."

Rosey shook her head and turned toward the bar. "I couldn't. It's been way too long since I've been up on stage." Rosey looked at Hyde as he sipped his whiskey.

"Suit yourself then, darlin'."

Rosey shuffled in her chair before standing up and walking behind Hyde. "Asshole," Rosey said in a sarcastic tone before walking over to the stage. Once there a man stopped her.

"Sorry, ma'am, I can't let you on stage."

Rosey crossed her arms and sighed. "You won't let this little lady sing for just this one night?"

The man looked around and was about to say no until the band leader stopped him.

"We'd love to have a female voice join us." The man's voice was rough and scratchy, probably from a mix of singing and smoking. Rosey smiled and walked up on stage and straight to the mic. Hyde turned his attention to the stage and watched as Rosey carefully put her hand on the mic.

"You'll all have to forgive me if I don't sound the best. It's been a while since I've sang."

The band got ready to play as Rosey took a deep breath. Slowly the pianist began to tap away at the piano keys, creating a beautiful yet dark melody that filled the air. Soon the saxophone player chimed in, adding to the dark melody of the band. Rosey closed her eyes and smiled as the music moved her and soon the words began to flow like a creak.

"All alone, in a city so dark." The bar turned in and focused on Rosey. "Lost in the violence drowning in a sea of bloody bullets." Rosey opened her eyes and ran her fingers down the mic moving her body to the music. "Lay down with me. Play dead with me, baby." The music picked up as the male singer tuned in with Rosey.

"Walkin' down the street street, all alone in the rain-ain." The man's rough voice balanced perfectly with Rosey's smoother, more gentle tone.

"All alone in a city so silent, all we hear is the violence," Rosey sang back, letting her hands trace her body for the crowd. Hyde sipped his whiskey as he listened to Rosey and felt his worries ease away. Her voice felt like magic to Hyde's ears. Rosey and the male singer finished the song and listened to the crowd's applause. Rosey took a bow before walking off the stage and back to Hyde.

"How was I?" Rosey sat next to Hyde and started catching her breath.

"You sounded amazing, Rosey," Hyde said before finishing his drink. Rosey smiled and sipped her drink as the sound of a phone began to break through the noise of the crowd.

Jack the bartender walked over to Hyde after answering the phone and tapped the counter in front of him.

"Someone's asking for you on the line, Hyde," Jack said as he cut the tip of his cigar off.

Hyde sighed and stood up from his seat.

"Get another double ready, okay, Jackie boy? Thanks." Hyde walked over to the phone as Jack got his drink ready. "Hyde speaking," Hyde said as he placed the phone to his ear.

"Evenin', Mr. Hyde. I just want to start this off by apologising for my associates the other night." The voice from the other end of the line was smooth and deep; it sounded more akin to a dull growl instead of a man's voice.

"It's no trouble, honestly. No one got hurt, but what can I do for ya?" Hyde said as he placed a cigarette in between his lips while Rosey walked up to him.

"Well, it's rather simple, Mr. Hyde. You see." The man on the other side of the line chuckled softly and Hyde heard the sound of a lighter being ignited. "You were recently in contact with a Mrs. Tina Lynn, and I need you to stop that." The man stopped and Hyde heard him take a long drag from a possible cigar or cigarette. "Just ignore whatever job she gave you for me, okay, or else my associates will have to get rough with you, got it?"

Hyde chuckled once the man was done talking. "Sorry, but I'm not on your payroll and your associates aren't of any concern to me." Hyde hung up the phone and lit his cigarette as he turned toward Rosey. "Come on, I think the girl who gave us the job is in some serious shit."

Rosey nodded and followed Hyde out to the car. Hyde sat down in the driver's seat as smoke slowly wisped out from his lips.

"What makes you think she's in danger?" Rosey said as Hyde started to drive off. That same distant yet determined look was in his eyes.

Hyde pulled out the paper and looked at it. Surprisingly Lynn had written her address down as well as her number. Hyde gripped the wheel tightly as he sped toward Lynn's home. As he drove, he heard a familiar voice in the back of his mind.

"Hurry, baby, don't be late again," the femaine voice whispered in Hyde's ear over and over again. Finally he snapped out of it as Rosey grabbed his arm.

"Will you talk to me? You went all serious detective on me again." Rosey looked Hyde up and down as he rubbed his head.

"Sorry, I've just got one of those feelings in my gut again."

Rosey nodded and adjusted herself in the seat as Hyde drove. After some time Hyde and Rosey made it to Lynn's house. It was a tall dark red brick building just outside the big city. The front yard was filled with many old stone statues of various things such as gnomes and gargoyles. Hyde got out of the car and held his hat as a sharp gust of wind charged into him.

"Stay here, Rosey," Hyde said as he closed the door and began to walk to Lynn's front door. The closer Hyde got to the door, the clearer the sound of gentle classical music could be heard from the otherside of the brick walls. Hyde reached the front door and looked at the stone lion that held a rusted metal ring in between its exposed teeth. Carefully Hyde grabbed the ring and slammed it against the dark purple door before waiting for an answer.

Several minutes later the door opened slowly and standing behind it was Lynn. She wore a short black evening gown with a lace pattern covering her cleavage. Lynn smiled as she looked up at Hyde before speaking.

"Oh, Mr. Hyde, what a pleasant surprise. Do you have any information on the case?" Lynn spoke softly. Her words flew into Hyde's ears like a gentle breeze and rested carefully in his head. As Lynn finished her sentence, wind blew between them, causing her to shiver.

"Goodness, um, Mr. Hyde, would we be able to talk inside my home? It's rather cold out here for me." Lynn's fingers wrapped around her door gently as she waited for his answer.

"Yeah, that's okay. I just have a few follow up questions I'd like to ask you before I get fully started on the job." Hyde's head felt light as he followed Lynn inside.

Hyde looked Lynn's body up and down as he walked behind her. The black silk gown hugged her body nicely, showing the world every curve she had. Lynn sat down on a large black couch with scarlett red cushions placed on top of it.

"So what questions do you have for me, Detective?" Lynn pulled a small purple cigarette case out from between her breasts and watched as Hyde sat across from her on a chair that matched her couch.

"You had said your husband was a gambler. Were there any casinos he'd visit more often than others?" Hyde couldn't shake the feeling that something was wrong as he talked to Lynn. He kept waiting for something to happen.

Lynn lit a cigarette and slowly inhaled the smoke as she thought. "My husband's favorite casino, unfortunately, was The Red Devil. He was always throwing away our money there." Lynn sighed, causing the smoke in her lungs to slowly creep out from her lips, still covered in their black paint. Hyde watched as the smoke snaked around in the air before fading away into nothing.

"The Red Devil, huh?" Hyde wrote down in his notepad as Lynn got up from the couch.

"It's scary not having him around anymore." Lynn held herself as she stood by Hyde watching as he stood up from his seat. "No one here at night to hold me." Lynn touched Hyde's arm gently. As her fingers gripped Hyde's arm, her soft words began to feel more akin to a viper's venom.

Hyde put a hand on Lynn's and looked down at her. "Let's wait till after I stop you from getting killed," Hyde said, looking down at Lynn, still feeling her words clawing at his heart.

Hyde went to turn around as the front door was kicked open and machine gun fire filled the room. Lynn and Hyde ducked behind a couch quickly as the deafening sound of the machine gun eventually died off and was replaced by the voice of a man.

"Find the girl. The boss wants her alive. If the cop's here, kill him."

Hyde sighed as he pulled his revolver out. "Nights like this make me happy whiskey was invented." Lynn grabbed Hyde's arm and shook in fear as Hyde looked at his revolver. "Stay here."

Hyde put his revolver away and stood up. As he stood up he put his hands up. "Gentlemen, I'm guessing you're not here for a late-night drink."

The guy with the machine gun aimed at Hyde and called out to the other two. "HE'S DOWN HERE, BOYS!"

Hyde smiled as he quickly grabbed the chair he was sitting in and threw it at the guy in front of him before running into the kitchen. The guy dodged the chair and fired a few rounds off at the kitchen door.

"Who throws a fucking chair durning a gun fight?" the guy said as he reloaded his gun while the other two went into the kitchen.

"Come out, come out, wherever you are, ya bastard," one of the men said as he tapped his bat against his palm.

"Yeah, yeah, come on, little piggy. Oink, oink. He-he," the other one said, holding his pistol while looking around. Hyde smiled and called out.

"I'm right here, assholes." Hyde stood up and aimed at the two guys and started pulling the trigger. The one with the bat dropped behind some cabinets while the other guy's blood covered the walls like a crimson rain. Hyde watched as his body dropped before ducking to reload.

"YOU FUCKER!" the man yelled as he charged to where Hyde was. As he did the other guy looked around for Lynn.

"Come on, little lady. The boss needs to talk to you."

Lynn covered her mouth as fear filled her body. The guy looked around and soon found Lynn hiding by the couch. "There ya are." He quickly grabbed Lynn by the hair and pulled her to her feet. Lynn grunted in pain and struggled before opening her eyes slightly and looking at the guy.

"You don't have to be so rough." Lynn touched the guy's arm

and smiled as his grip on her hair loosened. "Atta boy, just loosen up for me and I'll come willingly."

The guy let go of Lynn's hair and she quickly ducked down. As she did, she yelled out to Hyde, "SHOOT THE BASTARD!"

Hyde pulled the hammer back on his revolver and shot a few new holes into the guy's chest. When the guy's body hit the floor, Hyde walked up to Lynn and helped her to her feet.

"Are you okay?" Hyde said as he put his revolver away and pulled out his dented pack of cigarettes. "Son of a bitch," Hyde said under his breath, looking at his broken cigarettes.

"Yeah, I'm okay. Head hurts a little, but nothing this lady hasn't been through." Lynn rubbed her head and gave a weak smile before fainting. Hyde lunged forward and grabbed Lynn before she hit the floor. Hyde picked Lynn up and hung her body over his shoulder as he left her house.

"Goddamn this job." Hyde got back to the car and Rosey quickly got out.

"Jesus Christ, I thought we were doing a check up, not a fucking kidnapping."

Hyde gave Rosey a sarcastic laugh as he opened the back door and gently laid Lynn down on the back seat.

"Rosey, meet Lynn. She's the one who gave us the job. She's also connected to that guy we met at the warehouse." Rosey looked at Lynn as Hyde closed the door and leaned against the car. "This job just became a lot more trouble than it's probably worth." Hyde sighed and rubbed his neck as Rosey handed him a cigarette.

"You look like you need this." Rosey smiled as she leaned against the car next to Hyde. She watched as Hyde took the cigarette and lit it with his usual snap as he placed it between his lips.

"Thanks, Rosey," Hyde said in a muffled tone due to the cigarette staying in his mouth.

Rosey looked at Hyde and saw a growing red stain forming on his side. "Hyde, you're bleeding!" Rosey looked at Hyde as his eyes fluttered weakly.

"I-it's nothing." The cigarette dropped from Hyde's lips as he fell to his knees. Rosey quickly knelt down and stopped Hyde from falling onto his face.

"Shit, don't you fucking die on me, asshole." Rosey struggled getting Hyde into the car, tears trailing down her cheeks as she drove back to the apartment. "I'm gonna get you home and call Alan. He'll patch you up like always, okay, Hyde? Just stay with me."

Hyde drifted in and out of consciousness, the dark inky void of death loomed over him like a heavy blanket. The streetlights were nothing but dim stars in his fading eyesight.

"R-Rosey," Hyde said weakly as he tried to muster up the strength to speak. "I'm sorry."

Rosey quickly cut Hyde off. "Don't give me that bullshit. You're fucking fine."

Rosey parked the car and quickly ran outside and opened the door for Hyde. Thunder broke the silence of the night as lightning split the sky apart. Rosey had Hyde lean against her and before she left, she looked back at Lynn, who was still asleep in the car. "I'll be back for you."

Rosey carried Hyde inside and set him down gently on the couch before rushing over to Hyde's desk and quickly grabbing the phone.

"He better fucking pick up." Rosey's breath was spastic and quick as she quickly dialed a number on the phone. It wasn't long before she heard a familiar voice.

"Dr. Clyde, how can I help you?"

Rosey's voice cracked as she struggled to get the sentence out. "Alan, it's Hyde. He got shot and he's bleeding out. Please hurry." Rosey hung up and looked at Hyde. His chest slowly rose and fell as he looked up at the ceiling, occasionally grunting in pain from moving the wrong way. "I'll be back. I gotta get that broad out of my car."

Hyde's vision grew dark as he drifted further into unconsciousness. As the darkness wrapped it's grim arms around him Hyde saw that woman once again. She wore a long black dress this time with long black silk gloves to match. The woman walked up to Hyde slowly, her dark hair still covering her eyes.

Hyde felt her gentle hands caress his face as she leaned in close to him.

"Don't die on me yet. We still have so much to do." The woman began to giggle softly before she pulled back slowly. Hyde looked up at the woman as she slowly leaned in to kiss him. Before their lips touched, the woman moved her hair and Hyde looked into her blood-red eyes. Star-shaped pupils rested in the center of her evil stare.

Hyde quickly shot awake. Sweat covered his body as his heart raced. Hyde rubbed his neck before touching the bandages that wrapped around his abdomen.

"Morning, Hyde," a calm voice called out from the side of his room. Hyde looked to where the voice came from and saw a man standing in a long white lab coat. Smoke wisped around the man's head as he turned around to face Hyde.

"Morning, Alan, to what do I owe the pleasure?"

Alan walked up to Hyde as he stood up from his bed. "Supernatural or not, that wound was bad and you shouldn't be moving around yet."

"I appreciate you stitching me up, Doc, but I still have a job to do." Hyde grabbed a clean black shirt from off a chair in his room and put it on with a pained grunt as he left his room.

"Hyde, what're you doing up?" Rosey ran up to Hyde, leaving Lynn alone on the couch.

"Don't worry about that. What's wrong with her?"

"She's had a fever since last night, as well as something you might be interested in." Alan walked up to Lynn and tilted her head exposing her neck. "This also showed up last night." Hyde walked over to the couch and looked at Lynn's neck. On the side of her neck was a black circle with a red X over it.

"Mean anything to you?" Alan stepped back and exhaled a cloud of smoke into the air.

"Yeah, it's a seal." Hyde touched the mark before stepping back. "Rosey, get my jacket and my gun."

"Where the fuck do you think you're going?" Rosey said with her arms crossed. Hyde grabbed his hat off his desk and looked back at Alan and Rosey.

"Red Devil."

Chapter Three: Red Devil

"Not with that wound you aren't, Hyde." Rosey grabbed Hyde's arm as he put his jacket on. Alan walked over to Hyde and flicked him where the bullet was in his abdomen.

"Ah shit, what the fuck, Doc?" Hyde put a hand over his wound as he looked at Alan.

"If that hurts, imagine getting punched there." Alan cleaned his glasses on his lab coat before placing them back on his face. "You aren't fully healed and won't be for some time now."

Hyde finished putting on his jacket and walked past Alan. "She doesn't have time, Doc. Any moment whoever hexed her could kill her." Hyde put his hat on and looked back at Alan and Rosey.

Rosey sighed and walked past Alan to get to Hyde. "All right, fine, Mr. Stubborn. Let's go save this girl." Rosey smiled and waved at Alan. "Can you watch her while were gone? Thanks, Alan, you're the best."

Alan nodded as he sat by Lynn and watched Hyde and Rosey leave the apartment. "Don't get killed out there," Alan mumbled under his breath after the door closed.

Rosey looked at Hyde as he walked. A determined fire had been ignited within his eyes, yet she knew he was fighting off waves of pain. They reached the car and quickly drove toward The Red Devil casino. The casino was on the farther end of the downtown area where most small time gangs and wannabe mobsters did their dirty work; The Red Devil was at the center of it all, breeding evil and hiding the misdeeds of the scum that crawled out from within its hellish gate. Hyde looked at the large statue devil that held the casino's name sign and a pit formed within his stomach.

Rosey walked up to Hyde, bumped his shoulder, and looked up at him with a reassuring smile. Hyde nodded and the two of them walked into the casino. The sickening smell of cheap tobacco filled the air like a toxic cloud. Rosey stayed close to Hyde and watched the people lose their lives to the trance of the slot machines and betting tables.

"Why are we here again, Hyde?" Rosey said, looking up at Hyde.

"Because he's here." Hyde looked around as he walked through the crowd. Rosey trusted Hyde and stayed close to him, her pistol held tightly in her hand hidden within her bag. Rosey suddenly stopped as she bumped into Hyde, and upon looking up saw that man from before with his arm wrapped around Hyde his hand resting on his throat. Rosey wanted to draw her gun but didn't know if she should.

"Hello again, you two." The man's words were like snakes on the hunt, smooth yet full of venom. "What a very pleasant surprise this is." Hyde shoved the man off of him and watched as his body swayed back into a relaxed stance.

"You're coming with us, creep." Hyde's voice was full of anger, yet his composure was still calm and controlled. The man smiled and held his hands up slightly.

"No, I don't think so, at least not yet." The man held a hand out to his side and looked both Rosey and Hyde up and down. "Care to have a little chat?" The man began to walk off.

Hyde quickly followed with Rosey close behind. Soon the three of them were seated at a lone table away from any commotion. The man clasped his hands together hiding his sinister smile behind them.

"Who are you and what's your deal? I've heard mobsters talk about a supernatural creep like you."

The man chuckled and looked Hyde in the eyes. "Alester's the name, magic's the game." Alester held his hand out to his side as blue flame engulfed his hand while he spoke before quickly dying out. "And as for the mob, I'm simply using them to acquire a few necessities."

"What do you mean by necessities?" Hyde put a hand on his gun under the table and kept his gaze focused on Alester's one black eye. Rosey watched as Alester leaned back in his chair and laughed; she hadn't felt fear like this since she was alive.

"I require certain components to further my grasp on the afterlife. You see, I wish to have the power to completely manipulate a spirit, truly push them towards being the monsters you and I know they really are." Alester's eye locked in on Rosey and his grin grew wider, exposing more of his sharp fang like teeth. "Even a pretty face like hers can become that of a monster."

Hyde stood up and drew his pistol after Alester said that and put the barrel right between his eyes. "You dodged before but good luck doing it at this range." Hyde went to pull the trigger but suddenly felt paralized.

Alester slowly moved the gun out of his face and stood up from his seat. " Now, now, this isn't the place to break out into a shoot out, now, is it?" Alester walked next to Hyde and put a hand on his shoulder and smiled. "I'll lift my hex on dear old Tina Lynn for now, but only because I think our relationship is going to become a lot more interesting."

Alester walked off, disappearing into the crowd. As he did, Hyde's paralysis went away and he let the weight of his gun pull his arm to his side. Rosey stayed shaking in her chair as Hyde sat next to her once again.

"Damnit," Hyde said under his breath before looking at Rosey and seeing how scared she was. "Come on, let's get out of here." Hyde gently put a hand on Rosey's shoulder, which startled her for a brief moment before she saw it was Hyde who had touched her.

Hyde and Rosey walked outside the casino together. Rosey stayed closer to Hyde than normal. As they approached the car, she finally stopped and looked at Hyde.

"What're we going to do about him?" Rosey crossed her arms and held herself as the cold air blew around her. "I'm dead and I was scared he was going to kill me, Hyde. I can't imagine how you felt." Hyde watched as tears trailed down Rosey's cheeks from her eyes. "Goddamnit, now I'm fucking crying again."

Hyde walked up to Rosey as she wiped her tears and pulled her into a tight hug. Hyde rested his head on hers as he held her cold body closely to his. He felt her phantom tears briefly touch his shirt before fading away. Rosey grabbed Hyde's shirt tightly and buried her face into his chest.

"It'll be okay. I'm not gonna let anything happen to you, Rosey."

Rosey pushed away from Hyde gently as she sniffled before crossing her arms again.

"Yeah, well, just make sure you don't make any dumb choices, got it?" Rosey looked up at Hyde as he put his hat on her.

"Yeah, I got it." The two of them got in the car and started driving back to the apartment, hoping that things had gone better with Alan and Lynn.

Rosey got out of the car after Hyde had parked and looked at his hat as she took it off. She couldn't help but smile slightly before putting it back on. Hyde followed Rosey inside where they saw Alan standing by the window, having a smoke while Lynn laid on the couch.

"Welcome back, you two. She's fine now that the seal is gone." Alan looked at Lynn out of the corner of his eye before turning his glare to Hyde. "Good to see you're still standing, Hyde." Alan walked up to Hyde and flicked his injury.

"Doesn't hurt anymore, Doc." Hyde lifted his shirt and started taking the bandages off. As he did, he heard movement from the couch. When Hyde looked up, he saw Lynn sitting up, blushing before turning her head quickly.

"Um, wh-where am I?" Lynn said, rubbing her head.

"Our place," Rosey said in a not-so-pleasant tone of voice as she looked at Lynn. Rosey walked over to Lynn and looked down at her as she sat on the couch. "What's the last thing you remember?" Rosey looked Lynn up and down waiting for her answer.

"Um, I remember being in my home and these men breaking in and." Lynn stopped and looked at Hyde as he walked up to her and Rosey. "Then you saved my life." Hyde sighed and rubbed his neck.

"Alan, can you get me a drink? This is going to be a rough one." Alan fixed his glasses and poured two glasses of whiskey. "Lynn, your case has recently become a bigger pain in the ass. You've seemingly become the mob's biggest target as well as a big target for the man who killed your husband." Hyde held out his left hand to Lynn. "Let me see your hand." Lynn looked up at Hyde and smiled as she gave him her hand. Rosey looked at her hand a. it touched Hyde's. He closed his eyes and exhaled slowly. As Hyde did this, Lynn felt her hand get warm and for a brief moment a small sigil in the form of a triangle with a black dot formed on the top of her hand before disappearing.

"What'd you just do?" Lynn looked at her hand before resting it on her lap.

"It's a protection charm. Any hex of lesser or equal value won't harm you." Hyde stepped back and walked over to his desk, Rosey walked over to Hyde as Alan did a final check on Lynn.

"So what's the plan, Hyde?" Hyde went to answer but stopped as his desk phone rang, Rosey watched as he answered the phone with a sigh.

"Hello, how can I help you?" Hyde said as he stood by his desk.

"Evening, Mr. Hyde. I see that since our last talk you still haven't gotten the message, so perhaps we should speak man to man." The man on the other line laughed in his throat before continuing. "Care to meet with each other, Mr. Hyde?" Hyde tapped his fingers on his desk and took a slow deep breath.

"Where at?"

"Just a small bar just before you get to the heights called Broken Stool. Be here in an hour." The man hung up, leaving Hyde to listen to the dull hum of the dead call.

"I'm heading out, alone." Hyde started walking to the door.

"You do remember I haunt that car right?" Hyde nodded and grabbed Alan's keys

"That's why I'm stealing Alan's car." Alan stood up from the floor where he was kneeling

"Like hell you are. You aren't filling my car full of bullet holes again."

Hyde waved his hand as he left the apartment. Rosey looked at Alan before rushing outside to stop Hyde. Hyde was standing outside Alan's car loading his pistol when Rosey stopped him.

"Since when do you just do things by yourself? We're a team or have you suddenly forgotten that?" Rosey looked up at Hyde as he stared down at her, his eyes as dead as ever.

"It's different right now."

"How is it different, Hyde?" Rosey cut Hyde off, frustration and anger filling her body.

Hyde took his hat off Rosey's head. Her hair had gotten slightly messier from wearing it.

"It's different because I'm talking to who I believe is a mob boss, and if he's in line with that Alester creep, I don't want something bad happening to you," Hyde said as he walked over to the driver's seat before driving off, leaving Rosey alone in the parking lot, moonlight beaming down on her softly.

Hyde gripped the wheel tightly as he drove to the bar, a sickening feeling filled his stomach and a familiar burning sensation started in his left hand. Hyde sighed and sped up in order to get this meeting over with sooner, upon arriving at Broken Stool

Hyde got out of the car and could hear fighting already. There were two larger sized men standing at the front entrance; both of them looked like they could kill Hyde with their bare hands.

"You Hyde?" the man on the right growled out from his muscular neck as Hyde walked up to them.

"Well, I'd sure hope so," Hyde said as he looked up at the man.

"Follow me," the man said again before turning around and entering the bar.

As Hyde followed behind him, he could feel a slight reminisce of magical energy coming from the guy; it wasn't enough to actually originate from him, but it definitely had Hyde thinking about what Alester said before.

"The boss is right in here," the man said as he stood next to the door.

"What can't get the door for me?" Hyde said as he opened the door and walked into the dimly lit room. Sitting at the far end was a man behind a desk, a dull orange glow emanating from the cigar he held between his teeth.

"Mr. Hyde, we finally meet face to face." The man's voice dragged through the air before getting to Hyde. "Please take a seat." The man motioned to the chair in front of him and watched as Hyde approached the desk.

"How, oh, what's the word I'm looking for?" Hyde rubbed his chin as he sat down. "Inviting you are, sir." Hyde's voice was full of sarcasm as he leaned back in the chair.

"Yeah, I do my best to make my guests feel at home." The man locked his fat fingers together as he blew a large black cloud of smoke out from his mouth. Hyde studied each of the expensive rings the man had on his fingers.

"I want to know something before you say anything." Hyde leaned forward and looked at the man in his cold, lifeless eyes, the eyes of a scared man trying his best to be brave. "You know anything of a man with white hair and an eyepatch?" The man's eyes widened before quickly settling.

"He's an associate of mine. Yes, we're helping each other out through some internal business." The man slid a case over to Hyde. "Cigar?" Hyde opened the case and took one of the small cigars out and cut the tip off before liting it with a match that was also in the case.

"So why target a poor girl like Lynn?" Hyde leaned back as he looked at the cigar. "A grieving widow who just wants her husband to rest peacefully seems kind of low even for you mobsters." Hyde starred the man down as he ashed his cigar.

"Mrs. Lynn has a few things both Alester and I need in order to conduct our business." The man looked past the glow of his cigar and at Hyde, who was hiding his face under the brim of his hat.

"So you send armed thugs to her house and try to rough her up all while your associate places a hex on her." Hyde tipped his hat up and let his glare meet the man's, hatred boiled within Hyde. He wanted nothing more than to fill him full of lead. "Thugs who not only damaged Lynn's home but shot me with enchanted bullets." Hyde leaned forward and studied the man's face. A slight hint of worry had washed over him, but he still kept a rather intimidating composure.

"You're a brave man barking at me like this, Mr. Hyde." The man stood up slowly and walked over to a small table that had a crystal bottle of whiskey on it and two tumblers. "Care for a drink?"

"No, I don't take drinks from strangers," Hyde said as he watched the man pour himself a drink.

"Suit yourself. It's top shelf whiskey." The man turned around and faced Hyde. "However, I didn't bring you here to drink and chitchat with." Hyde starred the man down ready to draw his gun if need be. "I need you to give Lynn to me."

"Fat chance of that happening, bud." Hyde stood up and looked at the man as he held his glass; his hand had a slight shake to it. Hyde only noticed from the way the ice knocked against the inside of the glass.

"Then we're done here. Have a good night." Hyde chuckled and dropped his cigar on the floor as he walked away. "I'll see myself out."

Hyde left the room and walked past the man from before; however, as he was walking, the man grabbed Hyde's shoulder and spun him around. Hyde drew his gun as he turned to face the man and put the barrel right below the man's chin. "Bigger than me or not, this gun is still gonna lay your ass out with your brains all over the ceiling." Hyde pulled the hammer back as he stared into the man's eyes. "Now get your fat hands off my fucking coat."

The man slowly let go of Hyde's shoulder and backed away from him. Hyde turned around then stopped. "Fuck it, they want me dead anyway." Hyde turned around and aimed his gun at the guy before pulling the trigger.

Blood sprayed all over the hallway as the loud bang coming from Hyde's pistol silenced the bar. When Hyde finished shooting the guy, he put his gun away and calmly left the bar. The other man from outside quickly ran past Hyde thinking someone else was shooting.

"I hate mobsters," Hyde said to himself as he put a cigarette in his mouth. "From their taste in smokes to the way they act." Hyde snapped his fingers and watched the smoke leave the tip of his cigarette.

Chapter Four: Betting Man

The whole drive back to the apartment Hyde felt a pit forming in his stomach. Eventually he made it back, and as he got out of Alan's car, rain began to fall around him. As he stood next to the car getting soaked in the rain, Hyde felt a gentle hand touch his shoulder.

"Hey, come on. It's raining out. You'll catch a cold." Hyde turned around and saw Rosey standing behind him, her cheerful smile and calming eyes staring up at him.

"Yeah, sounds like a plan." Hyde and Rosey walked inside together, and when they got back to the apartment, Hyde started to explain the situation. Rosey, Alan, and Lynn stood by him and listened to everything.

"So yeah, that's the problem as of now," Hyde said as he finally took his soaking wet jacket off. "With Alester and the mob working together, it seems that this job is going to be taking up a lot of my time."

Lynn bit her nail as she processed what she had been told. "What could they possibly want from me?"

Hyde put his hat on his desk and walked over to the kitchen to get a drink. "Alester could be after your magic."

"Magic? No, I can't do anything like that." Lynn held herself tightly.

"Bullshit. I knew it the moment we met. Your words are enchanted, aren't they?"

Lynn sat on the couch as Hyde walked out of the kitchen with a tumbler of whiskey for him and Alan.

"Okay, you're somewhat correct." Lynn sighed and ran her hands through her hair. "My charms work a little differently than most. I can only charm men, and in order for it to work, I have to touch them." Lynn looked up at Hyde as he walked over to her. "The longer I hold onto them, the stronger my charms get and the longer they last." Hyde nodded as Rosey walked over to them.

"You don't think Alester can steal a person's magic, right?"

Hyde shrugged. "Anything is possible when it comes to this shit. I barely understand how mine works, let alone his." Hyde sipped his whiskey as he looked at his hand. "Although when he hit me that day, I felt this intense wave of negative energy force its way into me, so I believe his and mine are opposites in a way."

Rosey looked at Hyde as Alan grabbed his keys off the desk. "You three have fun with this. I'm heading home before the wife busts my balls."

Hyde looked over at Alan before he left. "Be careful out there, Doc, okay?"

Alan waved as he walked out the apartment. Rosey looked at Hyde as he sipped his whiskey.

"What'd you mean you two are opposites?" Rosey sat down on the couch while Hyde pulled a chair closer to her and Lynn.

"From what little I know of my own abilities, my magic has a positive effect on the afterlife and as well as the living, which is why I can purify evil spirits and turn them back to their more pleasant forms." Hyde leaned back and rubbed his neck before continuing. "Alester, on the other hand, seems to use negative energy to enrage spirits and turn them into monsters to use against people."

"How does that explain the ability to just disappear and dodge gunfire?"

"That's the part I don't understand. Shit, I don't even know how I'm able to light my cigarettes by snapping. Shit just kinda happens when you're dealing with magic." Hyde ran his fingers through his hair and sighed.

"Is there any way I can help?" Lynn looked at Hyde and Rosey. "You two are putting so much on the line for me and I wanna help out in any way I can."

Rosey handed Lynn her pistol and smiled. "Ever shoot one of these?"

"Yes, actually. Before I married my husband I used to be a not-so-good woman." Lynn hid her face as Rosey stood up.

"All right, I suppose this makes us a three-man team." Hyde stood up and looked out the window. "It's late. We should get some rest. Lynn, you can use my bed. I'll sleep on that couch."

Rosey watched Lynn walk into Hyde's room. "Do you really think this is a good idea?"

Hyde shrugged as he unbuttoned his shirt. "No turning back. I killed a mobster tonight." Hyde sat down on the couch and watched as Rosey faded away.

In the morning, Hyde was awoken by Lynn, who was shaking him in a scared panic.

"This better be good," Hyde said as he sat up slowly and rubbed his neck.

"It's my husband. He needs our help. I can't explain it, but I think he sent me a message through my dream." Lynn tossed Hyde his shirt from the floor. "Rosey, if you're there, please show yourself."

"I heard you. Hyde, what'd you think?"

Hyde stood up and slowly put his shirt on with a sigh before running his fingers through his messy hair. "We need information on Alester, and your husband is the best place for that as of right now." Hyde buttoned his shirt up before continuing his train of thought. "Lynn, did your husband tell you any locations or any details we should know?"

Lynn rubbed her temples trying to remember. "He showed me an empty cargo dock and a number." Lynn bit her lip trying to think. "Thirteen. Warehouse thirteen."

"Let's go," Hyde said as he grabbed his jacket.

He, Rosey, and Lynn all got ready before hurrying to the car to start heading toward the dock. On the way there, Hyde felt as if Alester's cold stare was focused on him, just like at the casino. It didn't take long before the three of them were standing at the entrance to the cargo dock. The feeling in the air was paralyzing as a thick cloud of sinister energy hung over the area like a hellish fog. Rosey looked up at Hyde as he focused his gaze before stepping through the threshold and back into the viper's nest.

"The one day I don't drink when I wake up." Hyde looked back at Rosey and Lynn. "You two stay here. I don't know what's going to happen, but I'd have nightmares if you two ladies got hurt." Hyde gave each of them a smile before Rosey walked up to him and punched his arm.

"Like I'd leave you to get killed by yourself, dumbass."

Lynn walked up behind Rosey and held the pistol she had given her tightly in both hands.

"Yeah, and I'm the reason you're doing this. It's time I took responsibility for my actions."

Hyde sighed and rubbed the back of his neck. "All right, let's do this."

The three of them began walking through the cargo dock looking for warehouse thirteen when suddenly Lynn dropped to her hands and knees and began to violently puke. Hyde looked around as his hand began to burn once again.

"Is it Alester?" Rosey said, drawing her pistol and looking around frantically.

"No, this doesn't feel like him." Once Hyde had finished his sentence, he was suddenly thrown into the wall of a nearby warehouse. The thunderous bang of his body hitting the metal wall echoed throughout the still dock. Rosey turned back toward Lynn and saw her beginning to float up into the air. Quickly she aimed her gun at Lynn.

"Drop her now!" Rosey shouted as a horrific spirit appeared behind Lynn.

"Who are you to order me around?" The spirit's voice sounded choked as if it was struggling to speak. Rosey steadied her aim focusing on the spirit's body that was just barely visible.

"Hyde, you better be alive!"

Hyde coughed as he got to his feet. "You must be Lynn's late husband, I'm guessing?"

The spirit stared Hyde down, it's dark empty eye sockets focusing on Hyde's heart as he stood there taunting it. The spirit screamed loudly, shaking the walls of the warehouse and nearly deafening Hyde and Rosey.

"HOW DARE YOU SPEAK TO ME, DEAD MAN!" Hyde drew his pistol and smiled as the spirit charged at him, still holding Lynn's body. Hyde dodged the tackle and fired a shot at the spirit's exposed body. Rosey put her gun away and flew toward the spirit, tackling it through Lynn's body.

"You better not shoot me, got it?" Rosey said as she began to fight the spirit within Lynn's body. Hyde nodded and took a few more shots at the spirit.

"PATHETIC PESTS! YOU"LL NEVER STOP HIM!"

Hyde put his pistol away and charged at the spirit. As he did, he grabbed Lynn's forehead with his left hand and forced both Rosey and the spirit out of her body.

"Rosey, grab Lynn and get her back."

"Right." Rosey quickly grabbed Lynn and began pulling her away. As the spirit saw this, it screamed louder than before and charged the two of them, but before it could reach them Hyde blocked it's path. The spirit unable to move in time went within Hyde's body, causing him to buckle at the knees and yell in pain.

"Hyde!" Rosey yelled as Hyde puked up blood and struggled to fight the spirit. Suddenly after what felt like an eternity to Hyde, his body finally went numb and he fell to the ground.

Lynn woke up and looked at Rosey as she ran over to him.

"Hyde, are you okay?" Rosey said, pulling Hyde onto her lap. Hyde suddenly sat up and began coughing up white smoke as he struggled to catch his breath.

"Fuckin' hell that hurt." Hyde held his chest and looked up at Lynn as she stood in front of her husband once again.

"Lynn, you have to run. Alester won't be happy until you're dead."

"But why? What does he want with me, dear?" Lynn said, placing a hand on her husband's cheek.

"It's something to do with your soul." Lynn watched as her husband's body slowly began to fade away. "I will always love you, my darling trouble maker."

"And I you, my beloved." Lynn and her husband embraced each other one last time as he slowly left her one more time for the last time. "I'll always love you," Lynn whispered as her arms fell around her own body. Rosey helped Hyde to his feet as Lynn wiped away her tears and looked at the two of them.

"Thank you, Hyde," Lynn said with a weak smile and slight tremble in her voice.

"Don't thank me yet. Job ain't done yet." Hyde looked toward warehouse thirteen. As he did, he felt as if it stared back at him with cold steel eyes as lifeless as his own. "Can you two go on, or are you going to head back to the car?" Hyde looked back at Rosey and Lynn as they both stood side by side holding their guns tightly, each with a determined fire behind their eyes. Hyde chuckled and started walking toward warehouse thirteen with Rosey and Lynn close behind him. The three of them soon stood outside its metal entrance. A cold chill had a tight hold on Hyde's nerves as he reached his hand out toward the door.

"Hyde, be careful," Rosey said, gripping her pistol a little tighter as Hyde grabbed the handle.

"I'm always careful." Hyde took a deep breath before forcing himself into the warehouse. The metal door screeched open as Hyde passed its threshold. Rosey and Lynn quickly followed.

The air in the warehouse was thick and felt heavy in their lungs as they stood within the dark grasp of the warehouse. Hyde looked around when he soon heard a familiar voice.

"Good evening, my dear friends. I appreciate you bringing me Mrs. Tina. It really does save me the trouble of hunting her down." Hyde turned around and saw Alester floating off in the distance, his hand placed slightly over his mouth.

"You'll have a hard time getting to her with a bullet between your eyes," Hyde said as Alester appeared behind him and placed an arm around his shoulders.

"Aww, it's cute that you think that scares me, Hyde." Alester got closer to Hyde's ear and whispered. "If that is your real name."

Hyde grunted as he grabbed Alester and threw him over his shoulder. Alester laughed as Hyde knelt on top of him and started punching him over and over again. Hyde stopped punching as he watched Alester's body slowly fade into a cloud of smoke.

"Oooo, it seems I've struck a nerve with that one."

Hyde stood up and looked around.

"Show yourself Alester!" Rosey and Lynn stood back to back as Hyde yelled out to Alester.

"Aw, but where's the fun in that? After all, tag has always been my favorite game to play." Alester quickly appeared in front of Hyde and slashed at his face with his sharp, animalistic claws before disappearing once again. "Tag, you're it, Hyde." Hyde grabbed his chest as his blood stained his shirt.

"Hyde!" Rosey called out and went to run to him, but Hyde held up a hand to stop her.

"I'm fine, it's just a scratch. Plus it didn't even hurt." Hyde gave Rosey a thumbs up as he looked around.

"Well, if that one didn't hurt, try this one." Alester appeared behind Hyde and slashed him again then disappeared, only to reappear again and continue his attack, leaving Hyde covered in deep cuts as a pool of blood formed beneath him. Hyde coughed up blood as he struggled to stand. Finally Alester appeared in front of him and hit him in the chest with a blast of dark energy that sent Hyde flying into a wall.

"You're boring. Stop holding back already."

A loud gunshot echoed throughout the warehouse as blood sprayed from the side of Alester's head, causing him to stumble. The shots continued as both Rosey and Lynn fired over and over again until both their pistols were out of ammo.

"LEAVE HIM ALONE, ASSHOLE!" Rosey screamed as a lead pipe began to float next to her before being forced through the air toward Alester; however, the pipe stopped just short of Alester's body and simply floated in the air in front of him.

"Bravo, bravo indeed, ladies." Alester smiled, exposing his monstrous teeth. "It's been far too long since I've seen this much of my own blood." As Alester spoke, long rebar rods began to float by him. "Normally these wouldn't hurt a phantom; however, I've imbued these with my magic, so I hope you're good at dodging." Alester laughed maniacally as the rods quickly flew toward the girls.

Rosey got ready to get Lynn out of the way, but right before the rods could reach them they were blown out of the air. The metallic clank of them fitting the ground filled Rosey and Lynn's ears.

Rosey looked up to see Hyde standing in front of them, blood staining his favorite jacket and his hat was nowhere to be seen.

"Alester." Hyde's voice was full of disdain and hatred as he stared Alester down. Rosey and Lynn stood behind Hyde and got ready to fight. "You two need to leave." Hyde didn't look at the girls as he spoke; he kept his murderous gaze fixated on the madman that stood in front of him.

"But Hyde," Rosey protested but stopped as she got a better look at Hyde. He seemed like a completely different person standing there. "Come on, Lynn, let's get out of here quickly." Lynn nodded and followed Rosey out of the warehouse.

Alester smiled as he looked Hyde up and down. "You really should smile more." Alester cackled before getting blown away, his body slammed into a far-off wall, causing a thunderous bang to be heard through the whole cargo dock. Hyde slowly took his jacket off and cracked his neck. As his jacket hit the floor, black symbols started to appear on his left arm all the way up to his neck.Alester floated up to his feet and clapped his hands in excitement.

"Yes, finally something inter—" Alester was cut off as Hyde suddenly appeared in his face. Hyde's cold stare pierced right through Alester as he grabbed a fistful of Alester's hair and sent his fist into the center of his stomach. Alester coughed up blood as Hyde punched him over and over again before he finally broke free and forced Hyde back with a blast of his own energy. "See how it feels to finally let go, Hyde? Oh, she'd be proud of you, wouldn't she?"

Alester smiled as he slowly licked his blood from the side of his mouth as he stared at Hyde.

"You'll pay for all those you've hurt, monster." Hyde pointed at Alester as the symbols on his arm began to glow. Alester shrugged and looked into Hyde's eyes.

"If you think you'll be able to kill me now, you're stupider than you look, boy," Alester said as he pulled his eyepatch off, revealing his eye was completely black. Dark ooze leaked from his now-exposed eye, and as he dropped his eyepatch dark phantasmal hands appeared behind Alester. "Now then, shall we really begin?"

Chapter Five: Awakened

Alester pointed at Hyde and watched as the phantom hands rushed toward him. As they did, Hyde ran toward Alester, getting slashed at in the process. Hyde's left hand burned with power as he sent a blast of his magic toward Alester. Quickly Alester flew into the air and landed behind Hyde. As he did the hands surrounded Hyde and readied an attack of their own.

"I've dreamt of this day ever since I traded my eye for this power." Alester laughed as he spoke, his monstrous gaze locked in on Hyde. "Please don't die too quickly on me."

Hyde threw his left arm out to the side causing a blast of magic to unleash around him, blasting back Alester's phantom hands.

"I don't plan on dying anytime before you, Alester. Understand that." Hyde aimed his hand at Alester as he bit down on one of his knuckles, attempting to hold in his maddening laughter.

"Yes, yes, yes, do it, Hyde. Hit me with everything you've got. DO IT!"

Hyde's markings began to glow as a dark purple ball of magic shot out from his palm. Alester's phantom hands quickly flew in front of him in order to block the attack. As they did dark purple and black lightning sparked from the collision. Alester laughed loudly, throwing his arms out to his sides.

Hyde took this opportunity and quickly ran toward Alester. He went in for an attack only to be thrown back by one of the phantom hands.

"When are you going to cast away this facade and show me your true face again?" Alester lunged at Hyde and blasted him into the ground. "I mean, this you is so boring, Da—" Alester was cut off as Hyde blasted him into the ceiling of the warehouse.

Hyde stood up and spit out a mouthful of blood as Alester's body slammed into the ground. "Stop acting like you know me, Alester." Hyde aimed his hand at Alester as he stood up.

"Ugh, I hate to cut our play date short, but I'm needed elsewhere." Alester held out his hand as one of the phantom hands brought him his eyepatch. "Till we meet again." Alester bowed to Hyde and disappeared in a cloud of black smoke.

Hyde rubbed his neck as his markings slowly faded away, leaving his arm feeling numb.

"Damnit." Hyde coughed up blood as his vision blurred briefly. Hyde started to fall to the ground but was stopped by a familiarly cold touch.

"Easy, big guy. I've got ya." Rosey helped Hyde to his feet and had him lean on her.

"Thanks, Rosey. Where's Lynn?" Hyde spoke softly as he held his stomach and tried to stop his bleeding.

"She's bringing the car to us. What happened to you?" Rosey said as her and Hyde started to leave the warehouse and wait outside for Lynn.

"Honestly, I have no fuckin' clue." Hyde looked at his hand as his vision blurred once more before passing out completely.

Hyde sat up quickly and looked around. As he did, he saw that he was in a large field. Sunlight blanketed the green grass as a blue sky hung overhead with white pillow-like clouds decorating it. Hyde stood up and rubbed his head. His body felt warm and cozy, yet his head was light and foggy. Slowly Hyde began walking around the field until eventually he reached a short wooden fence. As Hyde walked up to the fence, he heard two childish voices.

"Come on, Sammy. You're gonna miss it," called out a young boy as he ran through the fenced-in part of the field.

"I'm coming. Slow down, you know I'm not that fast," a more delicate feminine voice called back to the boy.

Hyde watched as the two ran toward a pond and looked into the water. He walked up behind the two and watched as the boy pointed into the water.

"See! I told you there were frogs in the pond." The boy smiled at the girl as she stared into the water.

"Wow, they're huge. Just look at them." The girl smiled as she pointed at the frogs.

Hyde went to reach out to the children, but they faded away and the pond changed into a hill with Hyde standing at the top of it. The children from before seemed older now as they laid together on the hill staring up at the sky.

"What're you thinking about?" the girl said as she laid on the boy's chest and stared up at him.

"That cloud looks like a dog." The boy laughed as the girl slapped his chest and sat up.

"You're lucky I love you, dummy," the girl said as she looked down at the field below the hill.

"I love you too, Sammy," the boy said as he hugged the girl from behind. The moment was once again ruined, but this time it was from a horrid thunderstorm and sheets of sharp rain that fell from the dark clouds above. Hyde turned around and saw the boy under a tree holding the girl in his arms. Her body was still and lifeless.

"No, no, no, please wake up. Don't leave me, please, Sammy!" the boy screamed into the rain as he held the girl's lifeless body close to his chest.

Hyde once again woke up, but this time he was in his bed and Rosey was standing by him.

"Ugh, my head," Hyde said as he sat up in bed.

"You're awake finally," Rosey said as she walked over to Hyde and put a hand on his shoulder. "How do you feel?" Rosey placed the back of her hand on Hyde's forehead as he rubbed his shoulder.

"Like I've got the worst hangover ever." Hyde stood up weakly and swayed as he tried to stand.

"Easy, Hyde, you aren't fully healed yet." Rosey helped Hyde stand and tried to get him back in bed.

"I'm fine. I've gotta finish the job." Hyde walked out of his room and saw Lynn and Alan talking in the kitchen. Alan looked over at Hyde as he leaned against his bedroom doorway.

"Not this shit again. Get back in bed, Hyde, before you kill yourself."

Hyde chuckled and walked over to his desk. "I'll be fine. I just need a smoke."

As Hyde grabbed his pack of cigarettes, the smell of maple sausage and eggs hit his nose. "Is someone cooking?" Hyde said as he looked toward the kitchen.

"I am," Lynn said, holding a glass of orange juice. "Rosey told me you haven't had a real breakfast in a long time, so I thought I'd make you some eggs and sausage as a thank-you for saving my husband."

Hyde placed his cigarette in between his lips and nodded. "You don't have to thank me, but I appreciate the meal." Rosey helped Hyde sit at his desk after he lit his cigarette. "Any calls?" Hyde said as Lynn put a plate of food in front of him and shook her head no.

"No, the lines been pretty quiet," Rosey said as she gave Hyde a shirt and sat on his desk. Lynn walked up to Hyde as Rosey looked back at him.

"So what was that whole thing with you suddenly becoming all intense back at the warehouse?" Lynn leaned on the desk as she asked her question and waited for Hyde's answer.

"Yeah, Hyde, what happened back there? You have to have some idea about it."

Hyde stopped eating and looked at his arm. "It felt like something snapped inside me and I was suddenly able to fire my magic on all cylinders." Hyde closed his fist before Rosey poked his arm.

"Can you do it again?" Rosey said as Alan walked over to Hyde's left side and looked at his arm.

"I can try," Hyde said, unsure he'd be able to redo what had happened.

"Unlikely, at least right now," Alan said as he tapped Hyde's arm. "I don't know much about magic, so this is coming from a more natural point of view, but from the description I was given, it's possible what happened to you was a type of magical adrenaline rush." Alan stepped back and looked at Hyde. "Similar to when a mother lifts a car off her baby, and also similar to that, it's possible your magic may or may not be drained for a while, like how when a person acts on a normal adrenaline rush and becomes fatigued afterwards." Alan cleaned his glasses and looked at everyone. "But that's just my medical theory on the matter." Hyde looked at his hand as Rosey and Lynn got off his desk.

"Oh, and who's Sammy? You kept saying that name in your sleep," Rosey said as she turned around to face Hyde.

"I'm not sure honestly." Hyde rubbed his head as visions of the children flashed around in his mind. Hyde stood up and looked down at his hand one last time. "I'm gonna head to AfterLife. There's someone I need to talk to there." Hyde grabbed his jacket and looked at the blood stains on it.

"I haven't had time to wash it. I couldn't find your hat either. I'm sorry, Hyde," Rosey said in a defeated tone as she looked down at the floor. Hyde tossed his jacket on a nearby chair and fixed his dress shirt.

"It's fine. It was an old jacket anyway." Hyde grabbed his gun holster off his desk and hooked it onto his belt loop as he walked toward the door."Rosey, you comin'?" Hyde said as he looked over his shoulder at Rosey.

"Yeah, on my way," Rosey said as she jogged up to Hyde and smiled.

"Alan, Lynn, can I trust you two with something?"

"Yeah, of course you can," Lynn answered for both her and Alan as she wrapped her arms around one of his and smiled.

"Head to the library on Oak Street and ask for Carla. Tell her Hyde sent you two and ask her for the gift. Bring it back here when you have it and don't open it, got it?" Hyde turned toward the door after giving the orders and left Alan and Lynn to follow them.

Rosey stayed by Hyde's right side as they walked to the car. She knew something had changed within Hyde, but wasn't sure how to feel about it.

"Hey, Hyde," Rosey said as she grabbed Hyde's arm gently to stop him once they were outside. "You know you can tell me anything. I've got your back forever, partner." Rosey smiled as she looked up at Hyde. Her hair blew gently in the autumn air as she stood in front of him.

"Yeah, I know, Rosey." Hyde's cold response wasn't anything new to Rosey, but it still hurt just the same. She watched as Hyde got into the car and waited for her. Rosey got in as Hyde started the car and began to drive off toward AfterLife. The city was alive with the energy of the afterlife as Halloween grew ever closer to the present; even Rosey felt the change in the atmosphere around her.

"Do you like Halloween, Hyde?" Rosey said as she looked out the window at the passing city lights, the dull oranges and yellows that decorated the streets and brick buildings like industrial fire flies.

Hyde shrugged a little before giving his answer. "I don't hate it. I think it's a nice way for the dead to see their loved ones again."

Rosey turned to face Hyde as he focused on the road. "Are you looking forward to seeing anyone this Halloween?" Rosey hoped to learn a bit more about Hyde's past before he started dealing with spirits.

"No one's gonna come see me unless they want me dead."

Hyde parked the car and placed a cigarette in his mouth. "Plus I don't remember anyone in my family."

Hyde got out of the car with Rosey, and the two of them walked into The AfterLife motel. Hyde walked up to the front desk and rang the bell three times in quick succession; after the third ring a black key appeared next to the dull out-of-tune bell. Hyde slid the key off the desk and into his palm before walking away.

"What are we doing exactly?" Rosey said, trying to keep up with Hyde's faster pace.

"We're hopefully going to get the edge on Alester for the next time we meet." Hyde gripped the key tightly. He felt the teeth of it digging their way into his hand as his grip tightened. Eventually they reached a dark purple door with dimly lit purple candles on each of its sides. Hyde held the key out to the door and watched as it flew into the lock and slowly turned with a gentle clicking sound. Hyde opened the door slowly before walking inside with Rosey behind him.

"Hey, it's Hyde. Are you in, Lil?" Hyde looked around before dim purple flames lit around a table in the middle of the dark room. Hyde approached the table with Rosey close behind.

"Take a seat, darling," a gentle voice called out to Hyde as the chair in front of Hyde slowly slid away from the table. "You too, my dear." Another chair slid over to Rosey. Hyde and Rosey sat down as a beautiful woman wearing a black lingerie dress that barely covered her pale ivory skin approached the table. A black silk blindfold covered her eyes as her long black hair hung all around her hair.

The woman slowly sat at the table and tapped her sharp purple nails on the table as her light pink tongue snaked out from between her lips and gently licked a drop of red off the purple lipstick.

"Dear old darling Hyde, finally come back to my demon's den, I see." The woman gently held her hand out to Hyde and waited for him to take it. Hyde slowly took the woman's hand and gently kissed it. "And you must be Rosey Ann. It really is a pleasure." The woman held her hand out to Rosey and waited for her to take it; however, when Rosey went to kiss her hand, the woman moved her hand and gently caressed Rosey's cheek. Her long nails gently pressed into her cheek as she smiled. "You were beautiful when you breathed, but now you're absolutely gorgeous."

"Lil, this is urgent. We need your help," Hyde said as he looked at Lil.

"Oh I know, you wish to find a way to kill Alester Mclain." Lil smiled as she placed a nail on her lip and giggled. "I can see that your powers have been awoken as well, Hyde, I'm very proud of you." Lil leaned in closer to Hyde, exposing more of her cleavage to both him and Rosey. "I did always love late bloomers." Hyde leaned back and sighed as Lil looked over at Rosey and smiled.

"W-what?" Rosey said blushing slightly as she watched Lil stand up from her seat and walk over to her. Rosey followed her with her eyes only turning her head when Lil placed a hand on the side of her face to make her look at her.

"Oh, Ms. Ann." Lil leaned in close to Rosey, their noses barely touching as Lil smiled and ran a finger across Rosey's pale lips before whispering something to her and backing away. Lil walked back to the head of the table and placed her hands on it as she sighed. "Alester is a powerful warlock, but you can stop him."

"How?" Hyde said, leaning forward waiting for the answer.

"There are two ways to kill him." Lil held her hand out as a bag slowly floated into her palm. "The first way, much like killing any man." Lil giggled to herself before pulling a dagger out of the bag and continuing her sentence. "Stab him in the heart. His body is cursed, yet his heart remains intact; it's where he holds the deal with the demon who gives him his power." Lil gave the dagger to Hyde and watched as the bag ignited into a small purple flame before disappearing.

"And the other way?" Hyde said as he hooked the dagger to his belt loop.

"Turn his power against him; however, if you do this, you'll die." Lil placed a nail under Hyde's chin and lifted his head slowly. "And we both know that if you die, I'll be a very, very sad witch." Lil licked her lips slowly before placing a gentle kiss on Hyde's cheek.

"What'd you mean he'll die? Hyde can use magic too." Rosey looked at Lil as she stood up. "That doesn't make any damn sense." Lil stepped back into the darkness of her room before appearing behind Rosey and gently placing her fingers around her throat.

"What I mean is this: Alester gains power from being a very bad boy while Hyde gains power because he's such a well-behaved gentleman." Lil let go of Rosey's neck and walked back to her chair. "Now leave me. I have other deals to make."

Hyde and Rosey both left the room in a hurry, not wanting to get on Lil's bad side. Once they left the door disappeared and the key faded away in a cloud of pale white smoke.

"Well, that could have gone worse." Hyde rubbed his neck and sighed as he leaned against the wall. "What'd she tell you in there?"

Rosey shook her head as she thought of what to say. "Um, it was nothing. Just how she wanted to hear me sing again someday."

Hyde nodded as he re-lit his cigarette and leaned his head back. "I hope they were able to get what I need from Carla."

Chapter Six: Sacrifice

Hyde and Rosey left The AfterLife and stood outside by the car, Hyde's lips illuminated by the dim orange glow of his cigarette. Rosey watched the ash from it fly away from him in the cold autumn air.

"Hyde, can you promise me something, please?" Rosey said as she walked up to Hyde and stared up at him. Hyde slowly exhaled the smoke from his lungs as he tilted his head up.

"Sure, what is it?" Hyde said as he flicked the butt of his cigarette out into the street.

"When we see Alester again, please be careful and don't do any risky shit." Rosey put a hand on Hyde's chest as she looked down. His heartbeat was as slow as ever; it was the one constant in their partnership that Rosey could always count on no matter what was happening.

Hyde put a hand on Rosey's head and messed with her hair before walking to the driver's side door. "I promise."

Rosey watched as Hyde got in the car after giving his promise, and as she got in the car Lil's warning echoed in her mind.

"Keep him from destroying himself, darling." Lil's words played on repeat until the sound of gunshots pulled Rosey back to reality. Quickly she looked out the window to see a car following them and a man leaning out the passenger's side window firing a six shooter at her car.

"ASSHOLE!" Rosey yelled as she leaned out her window and began firing back at the car. Hyde gripped the wheel tightly as his hand began to burn.

"Grab the wheel, Rosey." As Hyde said that, he leaned out the window, causing the car to swerve before Rosey grabbed the wheel. Once Hyde was leaning outside the car, a few bullets flew past his head but that didn't scare him. Hyde smirked as he grabbed his left wrist and aimed his hand at the car; as he did a blast of magic energy flew from the palm of his hand and hit the car, causing the engine to explode and the car to swerve into a nearby street light.

Hyde sat back in the car and shook his hand as smoke came off his palm. Rosey sat in shock as she looked at Hyde's hand and noticed a black symbol was in the middle of his palm. It reminded her of the night at the warehouse and she quickly took her eye's off Hyde's hand.

The rest of the drive back to the apartment was filled with a tense silence between Hyde and Rosey. She wanted to know what was going on in Hyde's head but couldn't bring herself to ask him. She was too scared of what the answer might be.

Hyde parked the car and stepped out into the rain that had started to come down. Rosey walked up to Hyde and tugged at his sleeve.

"Listen, Mr. Quiet, I'm not sure what's going on with you right now, but I don't like it." Rosey crossed her arms as the rain pelted both her and Hyde. "I'm your partner in this shit and I feel that I need to know what is happening." Hyde put a hand on Rosey's wet hair and sighed as he looked up at the storm clouds. The raindrops fell onto him like the tears he never cried.

"Listen, Rosey," Hyde said as he looked down at Rosey. "I don't know what lies ahead of us on this, but I know it's only going to get us closer to finding who killed you." Hyde tussled Rosey's hair and smiled at her.

Rosey looked up at Hyde's smile; it had become so different from the first time she saw it. It was the smile of a man who was tired of hiding his feelings. Rosey leaned in and hugged Hyde tightly and placed her head on his chest to listen to the slow rhythmic beat of his heart.

"Don't go dying on me over something stupid like that. Got it, you big fucking idiot?" Rosey's voice cracked as tears left her eyes. Hyde wrapped an arm around Rosey and held her tightly as he rested his chin on her head.

"I don't plan on dying anytime soon." Hyde pushed Rosey back gently and wiped away some of her tears. "Now cut the waterworks, okay?" Rosey nodded and followed Hyde into the apartment building.

Hyde and Rosey walked into their apartment and saw Alan and Lynn sitting on the couch looking at a small black box wrapped in dark red rope. Hyde walked over to the table the box was on and picked it up before unraveling the rope.

"Hyde, what's in the box?" Alan said as he ashed his cigarette.

"Yeah, it gives me a weird feeling in my heart, like staring down a dark hallway or looking over a high ledge," Lynn said as she stood up and walked over to where Rosey was standing.

Hyde dropped the rope on the table and opened the box before pulling out a small wooden spike with red runic symbols carved into it.

"This is a hexing nail." Hyde held the nail between his index and middle finger as he looked at it. "It's supposed to amplify a supernatural's power if it can be amplified."

"And if it can't?" Rosey said, walking up to Hyde as he held the nail.

"Then it kills them." Hyde set the nail back in its box and started unbuttoning his shirt.

"Hyde, what're you doing?" Rosey said with a mix of worry and fear in her voice. "Don't do anything stupid."

Hyde chuckled as Rosey said that. "I'll be okay. I promise," Hyde said as he grabbed the nail once again. "Wish me luck," Hyde said before driving the nail deep into his chest, spraying his blood all over the floor. Hyde grunted as he dropped to his knees while blood poured out from his chest. Rosey screamed as she grabbed Hyde to stop him from falling.

"Fuck, Hyde, what're you doing!" Rosey said as she grabbed the hand that was holding the nail in Hyde's chest.

"N-no, leave i-it." Hyde coughed up blood before falling unconscious. Rosey watched as the runic symbols that were once on the nail started to form on Hyde's chest and neck.

Hyde woke up in a dark room where he was sitting at an old wooden table. Black candles ignited with a blood-red flame illuminating a hooded figure that sat in front of Hyde at the table.

"Why do you seek my power?" the figure said as Hyde rubbed his chest and sighed.

"Damn, that shit hurts." Hyde looked at the figure as the flames flickered. "Listen, I need your power so I can stop this really fucked-up guy from hurting innocent people. I tried doing it with my own power, but I just couldn't." The figure clasped its thin boney hands together as its cold breath left from under its hood.

"And what is in it for me if I do decide to give you my power?" The figure's head tilted back slightly, exposing its glowing eyes. Each one was like staring into an ocean of blood and lost souls.

"My soul," Hyde said quietly. "When I die, you can claim my soul as your own and in exchange I get to add your power to my own while I'm alive." Hyde held his hand out to the figure and waited.

"An interesting choice, boy." The figure grabbed Hyde's hand tightly. Its grasp was as cold as death itself, and Hyde could've swore he had gotten frostbite from shaking the figure's hand. "It's a deal. My power for your soul." The figure chuckled in a cold and empty tone before releasing Hyde's hand. Once the deal was sealed, a black crescent moon burned itself onto Hyde's neck.

Hyde woke up once again. This time he was laying on Rosey's lap while Alan and Lynn stared down at him. Hyde slowly sat up and rubbed his head and neck before standing up and looking back at Rosey.

"See, told ya I'd be fine." Hyde helped Rosey to her feet before buttoning his shirt back up.

"What was that, Hyde? What'd you do?" Rosey said as she touched Hyde's chest where the nail had gone in.

"I just got the edge I needed to kill Alester." Hyde looked at his hands before clenching them into tight fists.

"So you took a magic steroid or some shit?" Alan said as he handed Hyde a cigarette.

"Yeah, basically." Hyde looked at Rosey as he put the cigarette in his mouth. "Now I can end this job."

Chapter Seven: Bad Memories

A young boy and girl walk through a dense wooded area. The sounds of birds chirping and water rushing through a nearby creek are all they can hear aside from each other's footsteps. The girl smiles as she looks down at her and the boy's hands as they stay interlocked while they walk.

" Hey Damian, where are we going again?" the girl asked as she and Damian stopped by a large pond.

"Right here, Sammy." The boy smiled as he pointed at the pond. "This is where I caught that huge frog I showed you the other day, remember?" Sammy smiled as she nodded and walked closer to Damian.

"Are there any more frogs?" Sammy said, looking into the water.

"Not sure. We gotta go looking for them." Damian smiled before jumping into the pond, splashing water all over Sammy.

"Hey! You got my new dress all wet."

Damian popped his head out of the water and chuckled. "Aww, I'm so sorry. Here, help me out." Damian held his hand out to Sammy, but when she grabbed it he pulled her into the pond with him. When she surfaced, Sammy splashed Damian as he laughed at her.

"You jerk," Sammy said as she smiled. "There's no frogs in this pond, are there, you liar."

"Nope, I just wanted an excuse to hang out with you." Damian smiled as he swam over to Sammy.

The sun hung low in the sky casting beautiful oranges and purples across the never ending sky. An older Damian and Sammy lay together on the side of a hill holding hands as they stared up at the sky.

"Damian?" Sammy said, looking up at Damian as he stared at the sky.

"Yeah?" Damian replied, not breaking his stare.

" Can you promise me something?" Sammy said as she sat on Damian's lap and looked down at him. Damian smiled and placed his hands on Sammy's hips.

"Of course, I'll promise you anything," Damian said with a large ear to ear smile.

"Promise me you'll never love another girl the way you love me." Sammy blushed as she touched Damian's chest. "Promise me that if I die before you, the love you give me will only be for me and no one else." Damian held Sammy's hands tightly as he looked up at her. Her long black hair covered most of her face as it sat messily on her head.

"I promise, Sammy." Damian sat up and put a hand on Sammy's rosey cheek before kissing her softly on her deep red lips. Sammy held Damian tightly as they kissed on the hill.

"I love you with every part of me, Damian. Not even death shall do us part," Sammy whispered softly as she rested her head on Damian's shoulder.

"Not even death shall do us part, beautiful," Damian repeated quietly.

Rain poured down from the sky like a cold, wet blanket. The wind howled as thunder roared in the sky after every crack of lightning that lit up the dark stormy night. Damian sat under a tree in the field him and Sammy would always walk through. He holds Sammy's lifeless body in his arms, a bloody hole through her heart causing her blood to stain his hands as Damian cried out into the rain.

"Please wake up, Sammy. Please, this isn't what I wanted." Damian cried into Sammy's bloody chest as he held her. "Please come back to me, Sammy."

"Poor little, Damian," a man said as he stood in front of Damian, the rain drenching his expensive-looking clothes as he stood out in the storm.

"You," Damian said as he looked up at the white-haired man. "You did this! Give her back to me!" Damian yelled as he charged at the man, only to be stopped dead in his tracks by the man as he pointed a finger at his heart.

"Hush, boy, you know you're what killed her, not me. This is the price of the power I give." The man leaned in close to Damian as his sharp claw-like nail touched his chest right above his heart. "I hope when we meet again, you'll have learned the price that magic holds."

Hyde woke up in a pool of sweat with a pounding headache. Through his blurred vision, Hyde managed to get dressed and ready for his morning whiskey. As Hyde left his room, he was greeted by Rosey, who was getting ready to enter his room herself.

"Oh, um, good morning, I heard you tossing around a lot, so I thought I'd come check on you." Rosey stepped back as Hyde rubbed his eyes.

"Mm, good morning," Hyde said weakly before walking past Rosey. "I'm okay, just had a rough nightmare, that's all." Hyde poured himself some whiskey as Rosey walked up to him.

"I'm making coffee. Make sure you have some. It might help with that headache of yours."

"How'd you—"

Rosey cut Hyde off before he could finish his sentence. "Every time you wake up from a nightmare you have a headache, and your immediate solution is a stiff drink. Try coffee for once." Rosey looked at Hyde and handed him a cup of black coffee. "Careful, it's hot."

"Thanks, Rosey." Hyde sipped his coffee as he walked back to his desk.

"So what are we going to do about Alester?"

Hyde set his coffee down as Rosey sat on his desk. "We know he's working with a small-time mob, so if we work through them, we can get to Alester, and once that happens we can put this all behind us."

Rosey touched the crescent moon on Hyde's neck after he finished talking. "Ya know, when I first saw this on you I didn't like it, but now I think it's kinda cute." Rosey smiled as she pulled her hand away from Hyde. "It just goes against your whole tough guy exterior, ya know."

Hyde chuckled as he sipped his coffee "Yeah I guess so," Hyde said as he looked around the apartment. "Where'd Alan and Lynn go?"

"Lynn said she was taking Alan to go and do some research at her house, but I think she just wanted an excuse to fuck him." Rosey laughed as Hyde grabbed his jacket off a chair. "Oh yeah, I washed it for you, so there's no more blood on it." Hyde held the jacket tightly before putting it on.

"Hey Rosey, can you promise me something?" Hyde said as he walked back to his desk.

"Yeah, of course, whatcha need?"

Hyde put a hand on Rosey's head and as he sipped his coffee. "If something happens to me—"

Rosey put a finger on Hyde's lips. "Let's not think about that. Okay, Hyde?" Hyde nodded as Rosey got off his desk. Rosey looked over at Hyde as he sat at his desk, and as she looked at him she remembered how they met and how alone she felt before him. Hyde stood up from his desk and grabbed his keys as he did Rosey wrapped her arms around him and held him tightly.

"You okay?" Hyde said as he placed a hand on Rosey's head.

"Yeah. I just..." Rosey stepped back and looked up at Hyde. "Thank you, Hyde, thanks for everything you do." Rosey smiled as she grabbed Hyde's jacket off his desk chair.

"You should wear it," Hyde said as he put his gun on his hip. "It's lucky." Hyde put a pack of cigarettes in his shirt pocket and started heading toward the door. "Come on, there's someone we should talk to."

"Coming," Rosey said as she put Hyde's jacket on; it was a touch too big so she had to roll up the sleeves, but she didn't mind that.

The two of them left the apartment and started driving through the city, eventually coming to a stop at the city police station. The sound of the police sirens was enough to deafen any nearby sound as the blinding red and blue lights flashed on the cars that flew out from the garage.

"It's been a while since I've stepped foot in front of this place," Hyde said as he got out of the car with Rosey.

"Why're we here again?" Rosey said as she walked up to Hyde as he looked at the station.

"Information on any local mobsters that have started causing more trouble than normal recently." Hyde put his hands in his pockets and started to walk toward the station with Rosey following close behind him.

Once they were inside, the noise only amplified, from criminals yelling behind holding cell bars to cops testing out new batons on the more unruly scumbags. As Hyde walked deeper into the den of these blue wolves, he remembered why he left it all behind. Eventually Hyde and Rosey made it to the chief's office. Hyde didn't bother knocking and just let himself into the room.

"Hey chief, got time for a few questions?" Hyde said as he and Rosey walked into the office. Rosey made sure to close and lock the door behind her in case things got ugly.

"Ah well, if it isn't the best detective to ever wear the Water

Crest badge. How the hell ya been, Hyde?" Hyde walked closer to the desk and ignored the chief's question.

"I need some info on local mobsters that have an increase in activity." Rosey watched as Hyde grabbed the chair that was in front of him and was reminded of three years ago when Hyde threw a chair at a cop that had spilled his whiskey.

"Ah, getting straight into things, I see. Well, I'm sorry to say but that information is for WPD officers only." The chief leaned back in his chair, causing it to creek under his weight.

Hyde chuckled and pulled the chair behind him and walked closer to the desk. "Listen, you fat fuck, I need that info now or a lot of people are going to die."

"Are you threatening me, Hyde?" the chief said as he leaned closer to Hyde.

"Not yet." Hyde grabbed the chief's tie and pulled him out of his chair. "This is me threatening you. Now, unless you wanna see how fast your face can go through this desk, I suggest you give me something to work with." Hyde's knuckles cracked as his fist tightened.

"You might wanna listen. This door is locked so it'll be a while before anyone gets in," Rosey said with a smile.

"I'm calling your bluff. You won—" The chief was cut off as Hyde slammed his face into his desk, breaking the chief's nose in the process.

"I never bluff, Chief, you should know that," Hyde said as he threw the chief back into his chair, causing both him and the chair to fall back, causing a loud bang to sound off within the office.

"O-okay, okay, I'-I'll give them to you," the chief said in a muffled tone as he held his face. "The most re-recent case is i-in there." The chief pointed to the drawer on the side of his desk.

"Thanks, Chief," Hyde said as he opened the drawer and took the file. "Come on, Rosey."

"Yup." Rosey said, grabbing a gun off the chief's desk.

"Why'd you take that?" Hyde said as he and Rosey left the station and started walking back to the car.

"Why not?" Rosey said as she put the gun's holster on her belt with the other gun she had. "I think it looks good on me, don't ya think, Hyde?" Rosey said, posing for Hyde before he got in the car.

"Yeah, ya look beautiful," Hyde said with a chuckle.

"Ha-ha, very funny, no wonder you're single," Rosey said as she walked around to her side of the car. "Where to now, partner?" Rosey said as Hyde looked through the file.

"Sixth Street. We've gotta talk to a Mr. Lane." Hyde started the car and drove off as he drove he felt a large pit form in the middle of his stomach.

Rosey sat silently in the car thinking about Alester and what might happen the next time they all meet face to face again. Rosey could still feel his stare from that night at the casino and how he made her feel; she could feel her emotions welling up within her until Hyde snapped her out of it.

"Hey, we're here. You comin' in?" Hyde said as he opened his door.

"Yeah, of course." Rosey hid her fear behind a smile as she followed Hyde into the apartment building.

"Lane's in apartment 2C," Hyde said as he handed Rosey the file before heading up the stairs nearby him.

"What're we gonna do when we get to him?" Rosey said as she followed close behind Hyde.

"We'll see if there's traces of Alester's magic and if there are we'll take action if not we'll simply move on." Hyde and Rosey eventually got to apartment 2C and as they stood in front of the door, they heard voices coming from inside.

"Listen, I can't keep doing this!" a male voice yelled out in a broken and shaky tone. "I can't keep killing. Even the boss doesn't make me do this shit. You're sick!"

"Ah, well, your boss is under my hand, which means I own

you," another voice answered back to the man, and as it did Hyde kicked open the door and saw a black cloud leave the room through an open window. As it did, a voice could be heard from it.

"Kill them," the cloud said before fully fading away.

Hyde watched as the man turned to him, tears running down from his empty fogged over eyes as he drew his gun.

"I'm sorry," the man said as he started firing his gun at Hyde and Rosey. Hyde grabbed Rosey as he got behind a nearby couch.

"Shit, you okay, Rosey?" Hyde said as he drew his gun.

"Yeah, I'm fine. You?"

"Be better when this is behind us." Hyde stood up and saw the man run out of the apartment. "Shit, he's running. Come on, we gotta go." Hyde started chasing the man with Rosey close behind him. Rosey ran out the building and watched as Hyde tackled the man to the ground and put his hand on the back of his head.

"I hope this shit works," Hyde said as the symbols on his arm started to glow. As they did, Rosey saw a dark cloud leave the man's body and fade away in the air above him and Hyde.

"Are you with us, Mr. Lane?"

"Please don't kill me. I only did what he said because he threatened to take my sister."

Hyde pulled Mr. Lane to his feet and held him against a wall "I'm not gonna hurt you. I just need answers." Rosey walked up to Hyde as he held Mr. Lane. "Who were you talking to in your apartment?"

"I-I can't tell you." Mr. Lane started crying again as he hit the back of his head on the brick wall he was being held against.

"Just tell me so I can help you, damn it."

"No, you don't understand." Mr. Lane's voice started to sound strained as he tried holding it together. "He'll kill me if I say his name." Hyde let go of Mr. Lane and watched him slide down the wall and hold his knees to his chest.

"Does he still have your sister?" Hyde said as he looked down at Mr. lane.

"I think so." Mr. Lane held his face as Rosey walked up to him.

"I might be able to help." Rosey knelt down by Mr. Lane and put a hand on his head. As she did, she began to see in his mind. Rosey tried to focus and find answers, but his mind was full of a dark cloud of sinistar magic, and as Rosey pushed her way through she saw Alester trying to reach out and grab her.

"Shit!" Rosey yelled as she fell back and tried to get away from Mr. Lane. "It's Alester. He's in his head," Rosey said as Hyde helped her to her feet.

"N-no, I didn't say it. No, please!" Mr. Lane began to panic and tried to run away, but as he stood up he started to puke up blood and deep cuts started to form all over his body. Finally the phantom hands that Alester used on Hyde ripped out from Mr. Lane's body and tore him apart, spraying his blood all over the wall of the building.

"Fucking Christ," Hyde said as he stepped back from the mess Mr. Lane had become. Rosey covered her mouth trying not to scream as she did the same.

"This guy is a real-life monster," Rosey said as she dropped to her knees. The vision of Alester trying to get inside her head still plagued her whenever she closed her eyes. "Hyde, w-what're we gonna do?" Rosey looked up at Hyde as he wiped some blood off his face.

"He has to be stopped." Hyde tightened his fists as he turned around and started walking back to the car.

Chapter Eight: Showmanship

Rosey looked at the pile of blood and guts that Mr. Lane had become. She felt her very being quake in fear as to what Alester was truly capable of and if she'd have the bravery to go against him once again with Hyde. Rosey dropped to her knees and covered her face, Hyde walked over to Rosey and knelt down by her and placed a hand on her shoulder; as he did, Rosey started to feel her fear leave her.

She looked over at Hyde's hand and saw the symbols on his arm glowing as small dark wisps left her body. Hyde slowly pulled his hand off Rosey's shoulder and placed a finger under her chin to lift her head.

"It's gonna be okay, Rosey." Hyde smiled as he looked down at Rosey before wiping away some of her tears. "I've got your back and I'm not gonna let anything happen to you."

Rosey sniffled as she nodded her head and slowly got to her feet with Hyde's help and the two of them walked back to the car.

"Hyde, do you think you can kill Alester?" Rosey said as she stood in front of the driver's side door looking up at Hyde.

"It's not a matter of can I; it's more that I have to, Rosey. There's too many good spirits that I don't want to see hurt because of Alester," Hyde said as he pulled a cigarette out of its pack and sighed.

"What will you do after all this is done and over with?" Rosey said as she watched Hyde light his cigarette.

"After this I'll work towards avenging you, then I'll probably leave this city. Too many dead bodies in the street." Hyde looked down at Rosey as the smoke of his cigarette filled his lungs before exhaling it into the air above him. "Plus I'm getting tired of getting shot at, so I think a house out in the country would be nice." Hyde smiled as he looked up at the cloudy sky.

"That sounds nice," Rosey said as she walked over to her side of the car and waited for Hyde.

Once Hyde got in the driver's seat, they started to drive back to the apartment to regroup with Alan and Lynn in hopes of trying to form some kind of plan against Alester. Hyde parked the car outside, and as he got out a wave of nausea washed over him and his vision began to blur.

"Shit," Hyde said as he leaned against the car, trying not to puke.

"Don't fucking puke on my tires, asshole," Rosey said as she rushed over to help Hyde.

"Something's not right," Hyde said as he covered his eyes trying to steady himself. "We have to get inside now."

Hyde began to stumble toward the apartment, nearly collapsing a few times with Rosey close behind him. Rosey had Hyde lean on her as they walked up the stairs toward their apartment, and as they got closer Rosey began to feel the malicious energy that was attacking Hyde.

"Come on, we're almost there, big guy. Just a little longer," Rosey said as she held Hyde tightly to keep him standing. When they reached the door, Rosey opened it to see their apartment in total disarray. Blood painted the walls and the furniture was damaged. Lynn's body lay in the middle of the apartment, and there was no sign of Alan anyware.

"I-is sh-she alive?" Hyde said weakly, finally falling to his hands and knees.

"Yeah, she's alive, but barely," Rosey said as she propped Lynn's head on her lap and placed a hand on her head. "Alester was here. His magic is everywhere," Rosey said, trying to purge the dark wisps from Lynn's body. Suddenly Lynn shot up right and coughed up a mouth full of blood as some wisps left her body.

"H-he took A-Alan," Lynn said, holding her stomach. "I'm sorry, H-Hyde."

"It's fine," Hyde said as he forced himself to his feet. "Alan's a tough guy. He'll be okay. Alester, on the other hand, won't be." Hyde's vision grew fuzzy, but he didn't have time to be weak.

"What're we gonna do, Hyde?" Rosey said as she rubbed Lynn's back while she coughed up more blood.

"You two stay here. I'm gonna hunt this bastard down myself and get Alan back." Hyde grabbed one of the wisps as it left Lynn's body. "He's gonna have a hard time hiding as long as I've got one of these bastards." Hyde looked at the dark wisp as it writhed around in his hand.

"Please be safe." Rosey wanted to argue, but she couldn't leave Lynn alone while she was this hurt.

"I'll be okay." Hyde focused on the wisp and saw a vision of an empty ballroom. "I've got a location," Hyde said before quickly rushing out the door, fighting the urge to collapse from the pain he was in.

Hyde hurried to his car and began to speed off to the only ballroom he knew of in the city. It was an old building barely held together, so it had become a type of home for the many homeless that wandered the city streets and subways. Hyde felt the wisp getting more and more agitated the closer he got to Alester.

Eventually Hyde made it to the White Cloud opera house. Long ago people use to come here to dance and listen to the many opera shows that would tell such beautiful stories; however, now it's nothing more than just an old crypt of past memories haunted by those who flee from the evil veil that this city covers its citizens with.

Hyde rushed into the old decrypted building. A thick cloud of dust flew up into the air as Hyde threw the door open. The wisp clawed at Hyde's hand trying to escape his grasp. Hyde squeezed the wisp tighter, causing it to wail out in a quiet yet high-pitched tone.

"Where are you, Alan?" Hyde said to himself as he wandered the dark never-ending halls, carefully dodging the many pitfalls that had formed from the old rotten wooden floor. The musty smell of the mold-infested walls would've forced any normal person to turn around and leave, but all Hyde saw was red.

"ALAN!" Hyde called out as he rushed from dark empty hallway to dark empty hallway. "ALA—" Hyde was cut off as a phantom hand lunged for him and grabbed his throat. "S-shit," Hyde said as he tried to break the hand's grasp.

The hand held on tightly as others came out from the darkness to grab Hyde before they began to drag him through the hallways, eventually bringing him to a brightly lit ballroom. Laying on the stage beaten and bloody was Alan, and sitting in a wooden chair next to him was Alester.

"Welcome, welcome, Hyde. I was beginning to think you'd miss the show," Alester said as he snapped his fingers, causing the hands to disappear alongside with the wisp Hyde was holding onto.

"Let Alan go. He has nothing you want, Alester," Hyde demanded as he got to his feet.

"Oh, I'm aware of that. In all honesty ,I wanted Mrs. Tina, but this insect happened to get in my way and I was caught off guard by her siren's touch." Alester floated off the chair and to his feet before walking over to Alan.

"H-hyde, ge-get outta h-here," Alan choked out as blood leaked out from his head.

"Just let him go, Alester," Hyde said as Alan began to float in the air toward Alester's hand.

"Hyde, why go with that name? It just sounds so forced." Alester snapped his fingers causing a large gash to open on Alan's throat, spraying his blood all over the stage floor.

"ALAN!" Hyde screamed as he ran up to the stage, only to get grabbed by a few phantom hands and slammed onto the stage floor.

"You never learn, do you, Damian?" Alester crouched down by Hyde and tapped the back of his head. "There's evil within you. Why don't you use it?" Alester jumped back as Hyde broke free from the grasp of the phantom hands.

"You know nothing about me, you monster. Don't act like you do." Hyde aimed his hand at Alester as the symbols began to glow and dark purple lightning sparked around his fingertips.

"I know everything about you, Damian." Alester smiled as he walked up to Hyde. "I made you what you are, and I can take it all back just like that." Alester opened his arms waiting for Hyde to attack him.

"Take this away, you prick." Hyde dropped his arm and ran toward Alester, tackling to the ground and putting his hand on Alester's head. As he did, Hyde saw into Alester's mind.

It was a dark, cold place with no signs of life, just a never-ending ankle-high sea of dark red blood and the disembodied screams of the spirits Alester had corrupted.

"It's nice, isn't it?" Alester said from behind Hyde, causing him to turn around quickly, slipping and falling into the blood in the process. "A warlock should always have a place they can go to think in peace." Hyde got up and swung at Alester only to hit a cloud of black smoke.

"Where are you, coward!" Hyde yelled out into the empty void.

"You have some nerve coming into my head and yelling like you own it." Alester appeared in front of Hyde and slashed his chest with his claws. "I think it's time you left." Alester grabbed Hyde by the neck and threw him into the never-ending void. Once he hit the blood, Hyde woke up on the stage floor with Alester standing over him.

"You're a monster."

"You sound like a broken record." Alester watched as his phantom hands grabbed Hyde and pulled him into the air. "Where's that fire you had in your eyes before, Damian, back when you were a young, eager runt."

Hyde chuckled as he looked down at Alester. "It's right here," Hyde said before snapping his fingers, causing an explosion in the center of Alester's chest, causing him to fly back into the audience. As he crashed into the chairs, the hands disappeared, dropping Hyde onto the ground.

Hyde got to his feet and rubbed his throat as smoke wisped off his palm. "How'd that feel asshole? Huh? TELL ME!" Hyde aimed his hand at the area where Alester landed and readied another attack but felt a hand on his back and his vision blurred.

"Easy, Hyde, easy," Lil whispered as Hyde fell back into her arms. "Can't have you dying yet."

"Fuck off, witch. He belongs to me got it." Alester sent his phantom hands toward Lil, but they were quickly dispelled by a wave of her hand.

"Shh, you should sleep too, Alester." Lil blew Alester a kiss and watched him fall to his hands and knees, trying to stay awake while Lil disappeared while still holding Hyde.

Hyde woke up on a small black couch in a dimly lit room. His shirt was on the floor next to him and Lil was sitting by him, slowly dragging her sharp talon like nails across his stomach.

"What happened?" Hyde said as he rubbed his head.

"Shh, just relax," Lil said as she slowly got on top of Hyde, her nails pressing into his body just a little harder. Hyde looked up at her. That black blindfold still covered Lil's eyes and her hair was still a black wavy mess. "You've killed your heart. How sad," Lil said, putting her palm on Hyde's chest.

"I had to. I need all the help I can get when I fight Alester." Hyde's fists tightened as he went to sit up only to be pushed down by Lil.

"Easy, Hyde." Lil leaned closer to Hyde, her lips inches away from his ear as she held onto his shoulders. "I saved you back there. I think I deserve payment." Hyde felt Lil bit the lower part of his ear before he grabbed her hips and pushed her back.

"I can't ,Lil. You know that," Hyde said as he grabbed his shirt off the floor and moved his hair out of his face.

"Sammy still has your heart, doesn't she?" Lil said, running her nails along Hyde's back. "Is that why you sleep with ghosts, because they can't fall in love with you?" Lil whispered before smiling.

"It's not like that, Lil. It has nothing to do with love." Hyde stood up and put his shirt on as Lil sat back and watched him.

"The man lost in limbo, all alone holding onto the heart of a dead girl," Lil said with a smirk as Hyde looked down at her with anger in his eyes. "Don't look at me like that." Lil blushed and put a hand between her thighs. "You know it turns me on."

"Why'd you stop me back there? I could've won." Hyde watched Lil stand up and put her hands on his chest.

"I just wanted to try to get close to you once more before you die." Lil kissed Hyde's neck softly.

"I'm not dying anytime soon, Lil." Hyde pushed Lil back and started buttoning his shirt up as he left her room. Hyde walked through the halls of the AfterLife until he was stopped by Gracie. She seemed scattered and lost as she approached Hyde.

"Hyde, where have you been?" Gracie paused as she looked up at Hyde before backing up slowly. "You are Hyde, aren't you?"

"Yeah, Gracie, it's me. Who else would it be?" Hyde said with a slight smile. "What's wrong?"

"The other spirits and I aren't safe here anymore. There's this fog that comes in and takes spirits away from here. It nearly took me last night. That's how I got this." Gracie pulled her dress up to show Hyde a large black cut on her thigh.

"I'll take care of it, Gracie. For the meantime, just try to stay close to the bar. It's the most protected part of this building." Hyde turned around and started to leave the AfterLife until he felt a cold hand grab his arm. Hyde turned to see a scared Gracie as close to him as she could possibly be.

"I don't know what's happened to you, Hyde, but please say you'll save us." Gracie looked into Hyde's eyes as faint tears trickled down her cheeks only to fade away before dropping off her face.

"I'll save you," Hyde said before pulling his arm away and walking out of the AfterLife. As he did, he saw Lynn and Rosey standing outside both looking defeated and broken.

"He's dead, isn't he, Hyde?" Lynn said in a broken and scratchy voice. "Alester killed him, didn't he?" Hyde watched as Lynn's cheeks turned red as tears began to flow from her eyes.

"Yes, Alester killed him and I couldn't save him in time." Hyde felt tears well up behind his eyes, but he choked them back, causing his throat to ache. Rosey held Lynn as she cried.

"It's gonna be okay. We'll avenge Alan. I know we will." Rosey looked at Hyde as she spoke as if looking for reassurance.

"Yeah, I'll avenge him, I promise." Visions of Alan's blood spraying the stage filled Hyde's mind as well as where he went when he entered Alester's head. "I'll avenge him," Hyde whispered to himself before walking to the car with Rosey and Lynn

Chapter Nine: Deadman's Heart

Hyde started the car and waited for the girls to get inside. Lynn and Rosey eventually got into the car and stayed mostly quiet as Hyde drove off, only making the occasional sniffing sound.

"Hyde," Rosey said in a soft, almost sheepish tone. "How are you going to kill Alester?" Rosey's voice cracked as she choked back her fearful tears.

"By any means necessary." Hyde gripped the steering wheel tightly as he drove to the dock. "Before I kill him, there's some business that needs to be taken care of at the dock."

Hyde drove to a secluded part of the shipping dock where it was believed most mobs handled their secret business. Rosey watched Hyde as he drove through the entrance gate before parking in the shade of a nearby warehouse.

``What's the plan, Hyde?'' Rosey said as she and Hyde got out of the car.

"Yeah, Hyde, what're we doing?" Lynn said, following slowly behind them.

"We know Alester has something hidden here, and I bet some of these thugs know what that thing is." Hyde's fists tightened as he walked away from the car. Rosey and Lynn followed him closely, each holding their pistols tightly.

The wind blew around violently as the waves crashed beneath the dock. The entire cargo dock had a sinister feeling in the air like an overwhelming presence was watching over them. Rosey and Lynn stayed behind Hyde as he walked, only for him to be stopped by a large bear of a man.

"Hey, no fuckin' tresspassin'," the man said, grabbing Hyde by the collar of his shirt. The thug easily had a whole foot on Hyde and was twice his body's width.

"Apologies, but I need a few words with you." As Hyde said that, his fist flew right into the center of the thug's face. The crunch of his nose breaking was loud enough for even the girls to hear.

"AH, MY FUCKIN' FACE, YOU PRICK!" the thug said, grabbing his face. As he did, he tried to punch Hyde with his free hand, but missed due to his broken nose blurring his vision.

"Sit, boy," Hyde ordered as he kicked the thug in the back, knocking him to the ground. "Now then, be a good boy and answer some questions for me, okay?"

"Fuck off," the thug muttered from behind his hand.

"That's not being a good boy," Hyde said before kicking the thug in the face. As he did Hyde saw the thug spit out a few teeth as well as a mouth full of blood.

"Fuckin' hell," the thug grunted in a muffled tone due to his swollen lips and broken nose.

"Now then, try again. The correct answer is 'yes, sir,' got it?" Hyde smiled slightly as he looked down at the thug's bloodied face

"Y-yes, s-sir," the thug said in a shaky voice.

"Good, now then, your boss, what's his name?"

The girls watched Hyde interrogate the thug in a mix of shock and fear. Rosey had never seen Hyde this violent with anyone before.

"H-Hyde, don't you think that's too f-far?" Rosey said as she walked up to Hyde.

"Mobsters and thugs are trash and should be treated as such," Hyde said as he stomped on the thug's hand that wasn't holding his face, breaking a few fingers in the process.

"AHHH!" the thug screamed out in pain, causing Rosey and Lynn to jump a little.

"Answer the question and you might be able to save the rest of your bones from breaking."

"Anderson, Mike Anderson. That's who I work for." The thug slumped over as tears ran down his cheeks and mixed with his blood.

"Is he in line with anyone?" Hyde said, grabbing the thug by the collar and slamming him against the warehouse wall he was leaning against.

"I-I don't kn-know. Honest. I sw-swear." The thug held his hands up in surrender as Hyde dropped him to the ground.

"Where can I find Anderson?" Hyde said, putting his foot on the thug's head. As he did, he heard a gun go off. Hyde turned and saw a few other thugs heading toward him and the girls.

"Shit, get behind cover!" Hyde ordered as he and the girls ducked behind some crates nearby.

"Are you okay, Hyde?" Rosey said as Hyde got behind cover.

"I will be when all this shit is over and done with." Hyde pulled out his pistol and leaned over the crate to fire. When he did, a bullet hit him in the shoulder right as he shot a thug in the head. "Shit," Hyde said, hiding behind the crate.

"Is it bad?" Lynn called out after she shot a few times.

"I'll be fine. It's just a scratch." Hyde's white shirt sleeve quickly started to turn red as he shot at the thugs. However, as he did, a black truck flew past him to pick up the remaining thugs before driving off.

"Shit," Lynn said as she stood up and walked over to Hyde and Rosey.

"Hyde, you're bleeding!" Rosey said, grabbing Hyde's arm.

"It's fine. We've got a name. Now to do some more digging," Hyde said as he dug two fingers into his wound and pulled the bullet out himself, grunting loudly in the process.

"How do you plan on doing any digging after breaking a police chief's nose on his own desk?" Rosey said as she watched Hyde heal himself.

"We aren't going to the cops. Lil should be able to help us find this guy."

Hyde started to head toward the car with the girls right behind him. As he walked, Hyde couldn't help but feel like he was walking head first into a trap.

Rosey watched Hyde as he walked. The determination that once made its home in his eyes was gone now replaced with a lost sense of hatred and confusion like a child lost in a store.

"Hyde," Rosey said, grabbing Hyde's arm as he reached for the car door. "Tell me and be honest with me. Are you okay?" Rosey looked up at Hyde as he let go of the door handle. "You haven't been the same since that incident with the nail. It's like you've lost your heart." Rosey touched Hyde's chest as she stared into his eyes.

"I'm fine, Rosey. I promise." Hyde held Rosey's hand as she held it to his chest. "I'm gonna avenge you, Rosey. Don't think I've forgotten that." Hyde smiled as he looked down at Rosey. Rosey nodded then got in the car with Hyde. Lynn sat in the back, checking to see if her pistol was fully loaded as Hyde started the car and began to drive off toward the AfterLife.

"Hyde," Lynn finally spoke from the back seat after some time of silence.

"Yeah?" Hyde answered back, keeping his focus on the road.

"Was it quick?" Lynn said as she stared down at her lap, a slight quiver in her voice.

"Yeah, it was quick," Hyde said as he pulled into the

AfterLife's parking lot. "You two should head to the bar. I'm gonna go talk to Lil."

Hyde got out of the car and was soon followed by Rosey and Lynn as they walked inside. Rosey grabbed Lynn's arm and started to take her to the bar as Hyde walked over to the front desk.

"Let's hope she can help," Hyde muttered to himself as he rang the bell three times before grabbing the odd key.

Hyde walked down the dull hallways of the AfterLife waiting for Lil's door to appear, the key occasionally shaking as he made a turn.

"Come on, Lil. Where the hell are you." Finally after what seemed like hours of wandering around, Hyde found the dark purple door and watched as the key flew into the lock.

Hyde knocked three times before slowly entering the dark room. Nothing had really changed, except now a large black cat with piercing green eyes laid on Lil's table staring right into Hyde's soul.

"Lil? You here?" The door slammed shut behind Hyde as the candles around the room began to light up.

"Welcome back, Damian." Lil's soft voice called out to Hyde like a siren's song. "I see you're alone, so I hope that name doesn't anger you," Lil said as she appeared behind Hyde and ran her fingers along his back.

"I need your help again. Can you find someone for me?" Hyde said as he watched Lil circle around him.

"I can find anyone in this city, Damian. You should know that," Lil said as she gently ran her nails across Hyde's cheek. "Of course, as you know, nothing in this world comes for free," Lil said with a devilish smile.

"I'm afraid I don't have much to give." Hyde put a hand on his chest and chuckled. "Already gave up my soul for a bit of power." Lil sat at her table and beckoned Hyde over to her.

"We'll discuss the price after I find your person," Lil said as Hyde sat across from her.

"The name's Mike Anderson. He's a wannabe mob boss. I think he's working with Alester." Hyde leaned forward slightly as Lil smiled.

"Ah yes." Lil gently pushed her cat off the table before beginning her spell. "Fiends and devils of the dark, I call upon thee to find me the soul of a sinner." The candle flames around the room went from a dark purple to a violent crimson color as Lil focused on her spell. The sound of growling and yelling could be heard all around them. Lil's hair began to stand at end as her breath grew cold. ``Find me this sinner's soul, give me sight of him, my beautiful children of the night." Lil's head was thrown back as her neck cracked.

The sounds of her night creatures grew louder and louder as the table itself began to shake. Jars were thrown from the shelves and pages from books were torn out.

"A-ahh." Lil moaned out as she floated up from her chair, long, thin arms reached out to her from the shadows groping her body as she floated in the air. "Y-yes, I-I see h-him." The limbs disappeared dropping Lil to the ground, Hyde quickly rushed over to her and caught her before her head hit the ground.

"Lil, you okay?" Hyde said, holding Lil. As he did, she reached up and gently touched his cheek.

"He's in the Red Devil casino." Lil smiled as she slowly stood up with Hyde's help. "Alester is near him, Hyde. Be careful." Lil kissed Hyde's cheek softly before watching him leave.

Chapter Ten: Fatal Words

Hyde left Lil's room and watched the door fade away after he closed it. A sickening feeling rested in the center of his stomach as he put a cigarette between his lips and sighed.

"Shit," Hyde muttered as he snapped his fingers to light his cigarette before he began his walk back to the main entrance. The sound of the band grew louder and louder as he got closer, and eventually the faint sound of Rosey's voice could be heard. Hyde made his way into the bar and sat next to Lynn as they listened to Rosey sing.

"She's got such a beautiful voice," Lynn said with a smile as she sipped her martini.

"Yeah, she really does," Hyde said softly as he took his cigarette out of his mouth.

"She means a lot to you, doesn't she, Hyde?" Lynn said, turning in her seat to face Hyde.

"We've done a lot together in the ten years we've known each other." Hyde ran his fingers through his messy hair as he looked down.

"You're a good man, Hyde. A little rough around the edges, but you're a good man." Lynn chuckled before finishing her martini. "Did you find what you needed?"

"Yeah, and I wish I hadn't," Hyde said as he stood up from his seat. Rosey saw Hyde as she was saying her good-byes to the audience and quickly rushed off stage to meet him.

"Hey, Hyde, did Lil give you the info we need?" Rosey smiled as she tried catching her breath.

"Yeah, we've gotta head back to Red Devil." Rosey's smile quickly turned into a mortified expression of fear as Hyde uttered the words *Red Devil*. She was quickly reminded of being face to face with the monster that is Alester and how he managed to paralyze both her and Hyde with terror.

"Y-you're ki-kidding, right?" Rosey's voice trembled as she choked on her words.

"I can go alone, Rosey," Hyde said, looking down at Rosey as she bit her fingernails.

"No, I'll go with you. It won't be like last time."

Lynn stood up and wrapped an arm around Rosey. "Yeah, plus I'll be there too. Don't forget I'm a supernatural, too, Hyde." Lynn winked as Hyde turned around to leave the bar, the girls quickly following him.

"Here's the plan," Hyde said as the three of them reached the car. "We go in, look for our target, we find him, get the answers we need, and then find Alester."

"And if we find Alester first?" Lynn said, raising her hand in a joking manner.

"Then we kill him," Hyde said, clenching his fists in anger before getting into the car.

"Let's get this bastard!" Rosey said excitedly as she got into the passenger's seat.

The drive to the Red Devil was mostly quiet. It seemed the closer they got, the more the weight of what they were doing seemed to press down on them. A thick, dark fog covered the street as they closed in on the casino, and each of them could feel Alester's sinister gaze fixating on them. Hyde gripped the wheel tightly as Rosey and Lynn checked their pistols for the twentieth time before the car finally stopped.

The bright red sign that hung off the front of the building seemed to be calling in every mindless zombie under the casino's control; however, to them it was akin to staring into the eyes of the Devil himself. Hyde was the first one brave enough to step foot outside the car. The air was thick, and each breath Hyde took seemed like it was trying to choke him. Rosey and Lynn got out at the same time and both just stared up at the sign. The cartoon devil smiled down at them, fanning a stack of one hundred dollar bills.

Hyde cleared his throat and bit the inside of his cheek as he forced himself to move forward. Rosey and Lynn nervously followed behind him.

The casino was packed full of mindless people constantly feeding the machines their hard-earned money just to watch the bright colored lights flash. The sound of coins hitting metal and machines dinging was nearly deafening. Rosey and Lynn locked arms as Hyde pushed ahead of them.

"Stay close!" Hyde shouted back toward the girls as he shoved a person out of his way. As he did he saw a marking on his hand began to glow. "Please be what I think you are," Hyde muttered to himself as he shoved through the crowd. Lynn and Rosey hurried behind him trying not to get lost in the ocean of people.

As Hyde made his way into a clearing he saw a man in a dark suit sitting at a table with a few beautiful women. A fat cigar was clamped in between his lips and a dark smoke cloud hung over his head.

"That him?" Rosey said as she finally got out of the hoard of people, Lynn still holding her arm tightly.

"Yeah, that's our guy," Hyde said as he began his approach. "Apologies, ladies, but I need a word with my friend here." Hyde smiled as he pulled out a chair and sat in front of Mike.

"Beat it, punk. I ain't know you," Mike muttered through his fat lips that held onto his cigar.

"Oh, I know, but we're gonna get to know each other real well," Hyde said with a dull smirk.

"Beat it, gals. Papa's gotta do some tawlkin'." Mike leaned forward, his suit straining to keep his large body covered. "Now, who da hell do ya think yous is?" Mike said, pointing his sausage fingers in Hyde's face.

"Hyde, paranormal investigator." Hyde smiled as he moved Mike's fingers out of his face.

"Paranormal? What, like ghosts and shit? HA-HA!" Mike slammed his large hand on the table, knocking over a few empty glasses as he laughed. "Fuck off. I ain't gots the time to entertain a nutcase." Mike went to stand up, but stopped when Rosey put the barrel of her gun against his swollen cheek.

"Make time, then, fatass," Hyde said, clasping his hands together. "Because my patience is already paper thin with you mob freaks."

Mike sniffled as he sat back in his chair. "Big man, makin' a dame use the gun." Mike chuckled.

"He doesn't make me do shit," Rosey said, fighting back the urge to slam the butt of her pistol into Mike's fat head.

"Now then, answer my questions and you'll leave here without any extra holes. Sound good?"

"You've got some nerve, threatin' Big Mike." Mike fixed his jacket as he moved in his seat.

"You know anyone by the name of Alester? Creep with white hair, dresses kinda funny."

"Doesn't ring a bell. I work with a lot of characters." Mike chuckled as he stared into Hyde's eyes.

"I see." Hyde nodded his head before grabbing the empty wine bottle off the table and smashing it on the side of Mike's head, knocking his hat to the floor in the process. "That jog your memory?"

"You son of a BITCH!" Mike yelled, throwing the table to the side and going in to tackle Hyde; however, as he did, Hyde pressed the barrel of his gun between Mike's eyes.

"Let's not make a scene, shall we?"

Mike's eyes crossed as he looked at the barrel. "Perhaps a private room would be better."

"Y-yeah, good point."

Hyde stood up and got behind Mike, pressing his gun against his spine. "One wrong move and I'll make sure you're crawling out of here with broken fingers and a shattered jaw, got it, Big Mike?" Hyde said Mike's nickname with a laugh.

"Yeah, I got it. I swears." Mike started walking as Hyde shoved him.

Once they were in a private room, Mike sat down at the new table and dabbed his sweat away with the handkerchief he kept on him.

"Now then, Alester. Does the name ring any bells?" Hyde said, crossing his arms.

"Yeah, it does. Real creepy fuck with an eyepatch, right?"

"Bingo!" Rosey exclaimed, still aiming her gun at Mike.

"Yeah, my boys and I was workin' with 'im. He asked us to guard a warehouse on da dock for him, so wes did."

"There's more to it, though, isn't there?"

"I-I aint snitchin' on shit. I don't care what yous do ta me," Mike said, crossing his arms like a toddler.

"Ladies, please step outside the room for me," Hyde ordered as he loosened his tie.

"Yessir," Rosey said, taking Lynn outside the door.

"What're you gonna do, ru—" Mike couldn't finish his taunt. Hyde kicked the edge of the table, sending into Mike's large stomach before grabbing his expensive shirt and sending his right fist into Mike's pig-like nose.

Lynn touched up her makeup as her and Rosey listened to the fight. Five minutes later, Hyde opened the door as he buttoned up his shirt.

"Ladies," Hyde said, motioning for Rosey and Lynn to come in. The room was completely destroyed, the table had been split in half, and there was a broken chair leg sticking out of Mike's leg.

Mike was trying to pull the leg out, but all ten of his fingers were horribly broken; his nose was almost completely smashed into his face and his eyes were swollen shut.

"Now then, are you going to cooperate now, Mike?" Hyde said crouching next to Mike.

"Y-yes," Mike mumbled through busted lips and a dislocated jaw.

"Good. So what else did Alester have you do?" Hyde grabbed Mike's collar and held him against a wall after asking his question.

"W-we ha-had to br-bring hi-him pe-pe-people," Mike stuttered as he coughed up blood.

"Is he here?" Hyde demanded as he slammed Mike against the wall.

"N-no, h-h-he sa-said he ha-h-had th-things to d-d-do." Mike held his broken hands up to cover his face. "P-please, n-n-no mo-more." Hyde dropped Mike to the floor as he began to cry.

'Shit." Hyde rubbed his chin as he leaned against the wall.

"What now, Hyde?" Lynn said as she looked around at the mess.

"Do we hunt him down?" Rosey asked nervously as she walked up to Hyde. Hyde shoved Mike's leg with his foot to get his attention.

"Alester comes back here a lot, doesn't he?"

"I-I th-think so," Mike muttered through his fits of crying

"Then we'll take the chance and wait here for him. Take him down at the heart of his whole organization."

Hyde and the girls left the room, leaving Mike to cry his pain away. Once they left the casino, there was a sense of dread that resonated within each of them.

Terror filled each of their hearts as they sat in the car. Time seemed to slow down as anxiety filled the air around them. Hyde gripped the wheel as he tried to steady himself.

"Is this really going to happen?" Lynn asked, finally breaking the silence as she sat in the back holding her knees close to her chest.

"Yeah, it has to," Hyde answered back as he stared at the Red Devil sign. "If we don't end this, Alester will only get stronger.

He'll just keep killing." Hyde felt his stomach in his throat as he waited for any sign that Alester had returned.

Hours went by and the street grew darker and darker as twilight fell over them. The once brightly lit sign now lay cold and lifeless only being illuminated by the faint moonlight breaking through the clouds. The three of them waited, each one of them was as focused as they could be.

"Hey, look over there!" Lynn exclaimed quietly, pointing out the windshield.

"What?" Hyde said, looking where Lynn was pointing. As he did, he saw a sleek black car pulling behind the casino, and as it stopped out came Alester himself. Hyde's blood ran cold as he stared at Alester. They all watched as he and a few other men walked into the casino through the back door, and after waiting a few extra minutes, Hyde, Rosey, and Lynn got out of their car and made their way toward the back door.

Hyde moved slowly as he got closer to the door. Eventually he stopped in front of the metal door. With sweaty palms he reached for the handle. Rosey quickly grabbed his hand and looked up at him with a determined glance.

"Right," Hyde said before grabbing the handle and carefully opening the door. "Okay. Follow me," Hyde whispered before sneaking through the ajar door. Lynn carefully shut it behind them after she entered.

Hyde looked around the room they had entered. It was some type of storage room. As Hyde looked around, he could hear voices coming from a nearby hallway. Quickly he motioned everyone to hide. Each of them hurried and ducked behind some boxes and waited.

"This job's really killin' my sleep schedule, Mac," a voice called out as two men walked into the room.

"I hear ya on that. I always hated the night shift." The men walked around the room, eventually stopping by a large crate.

"Shit, is this what we need to haul upstairs?"

"Looks like it." The men sighed loudly before grabbing the crate. "Goddamn, this bitch is heavy. What's in here a body?"

"Just shut up and lift." The men grunted as they hoisted the crate into the air and began to carry it out of the room.

Hyde looked over at Rosey and Lynn and motioned for them to follow him. The girls carefully moved over to Hyde and watched as the men left the room. Hyde saw his chance and hurried over to the door, stopping it just before it slammed shut.

"Come on," Hyde whispered as he beckoned the girls to follow him. Hyde held the door open as Rosey and Lynn hurried out of the storage room, and once they were out Hyde carefully shut the door and looked around.

"Where are we?" Rosey whispered as she looked around.

"Looks like some back hallway for the workers," Hyde answered quietly before moving forward. The muffled sound of voices could be heard in the distance. Hyde carefully moved in their direction, eventually making it to a set of swing double doors. Cautiously Hyde peaked through the window in the door and saw it lead to the casino's main floor.

There Hyde saw the mobsters moving more of those crates, and Alester was talking to a very beaten Mike. Hyde focused in on them only to see Alester execute Mike in the middle of the floor. He ducked down quickly after seeing that and silently cursed to himself.

"What'd you see?" Rosey asked as she crouched down in front of Hyde.

"Bastard's got a whole army in there." Hyde grabbed at his chest as a stabbing pain pierced his heart. "And I've got a feeling he knows I'm here." Hyde leaned against the wall and chuckled softly.

Lynn looked out the window and watched as Alester moved toward a set of stairs.

"Looks like Alester is heading upstairs. Is there a way we can head up there from here?" Lynn asked as she crouched down.

"Yeah, these casinos always have rat ways for their staff to move around." Hyde stood up slowly before moving away from the doors.

The group moved around the back hallways, dodging mobsters and occasionally taking a few out if need be. A monstrous feeling of negative energy soon filled the air as they reached a staircase.

"I guess this is us," Rosey said nervously as she held Hyde's arm.

"Yeah, it looks like it," Lynn agreed

"Let's move," Hyde ordered as he forced himself to move up the stairs. Each step he took made the weight in Hyde's stomach grow heavier and heavier; the three of them each felt this weight as if Alester himself was pushing down on their very souls. They soon reached the top of the stairs, and as they did voices could be heard coming from the stairwell.

"Looks like some bodies got found," Lynn said with a nervous chuckle. "Look, you two go and finish this. I'll catch up after I deal with these bastards." Lynn smiled as she hugged Rosey and gave Hyde a thumbs up.

"You don't have to do this, Lynn," Hyde said as the voices grew closer.

"Just go. It's time I really helped out," Lynn ordered before hiding behind a nearby shelf.

Hyde and Rosey nodded before rushing through the hallway toward a large door. The sinister energy in the air grew thicker and thicker the closer Hyde and Rosey got to the door until it eventually felt like walking through a musty fog. Hyde reached out to the door handle as a pain filled his chest and wrapped around his heart. Rosey once again grabbed his hand, and together they pushed through the doorway and into the large office.

Occult symbols decorated the walls and floor as candles burned a bright crimson flame, and standing in the center of it all was Alester himself. The air was heavy and as the door slammed shut behind Hyde and Rosey, they both knew that there was no turning back.

"This ends here, Alester!" Hyde shouted as he walked in front of Rosey.

"Ah, you two. Yes, I must agree this does end here." Alester ran his fingers through his ash-white hair as he smiled exposing his blade-like teeth. "It does sadden me. You see, I had hoped that you'd join me, Damian."

"Damian?" Rosey asked in a confused tone as she looked at Hyde.

"Oh, he never told you, darling?" Alester cackled as he spoke. "Yes, dear old Hyde here is really named Damian; however, after the death of his childhood love and soon-to-be wife he changed it because he hated the way his name sounded coming from anyone but her." Alester stared into Hyde's eyes as he smiled.

"Cut the shit and admit you killed her, Alester!" Hyde ordered, the markings on his arm beginning to glow as his anger built.

"Oh, but I didn't. You did." Alester's words were venom to Hyde's ears. "You killed her the day you shook my hand." Alester held his hand out to Hyde as he spoke, only to tighten it into a fist. "However, dear Rosey Ann, I must admit taking your life was no easy task, and that car trapping your soul wasn't part of the plan either." Alester smiled as his gaze locked in an Rosey.

"W-what?" Rosey stuttered as her knees began to buckle. "N-no, i-i-it can b-be yo-you." Rosey dropped to her knees as phantom tears fell from her eyes.

"Ah yes, I remember the night so well." Alester spun around as he laughed. "Your show was beautiful. Truly an angelic voice." Alester clasped his hands over his heart. "It was then I knew your soul had to be mind." Rosey looked up at Alester as Hyde stood in front of her.

"H-Hyde, i-i-it's hi-him." Rosey felt like a scared little girl as she pointed a shaky finger at the demon that stood in front of her and Hyde.

"I know, and it's time I make good on a promise." Hyde's determination ignited within him as he loosened his tie.

"Come on then, Damian," Alester said, opening his arms wide with a sadistic demon's grin.

Chapter Eleven:
Bloody Hands

Hyde looked at the monster that stood in front of him. Memories of holding Sammy on the hill and meeting Rosey on that rainy night filled his mind as he walked toward who, in his mind, was the devil himself. Anger and hatred boiled within his very soul; purple electricity sparked from his fingertips and danced up his arms. Alester smiled as he walked toward Hyde, black electricity dashed around his clawed fingers, and soon the two were a mere arms distance from each other.

"KILL HIM, HYDE!" Rosey yelled with everything she had, and as she did Hyde's fist flew into Alester's face, only for Aleester to slash at Hyde's chest as he stepped back before laughing.

"Yes, Damian, come kill me!" Alester ordered as he recovered from the punch. "COME AVENGE THEM ALL!" Alester yelled in a demonic tone as several tortured spirits flew out from the symbols that decorated the walls and floor toward Hyde.

Hyde readied himself and began dodging the attacks as they came, attempting to purify any spirits he could. Sharp claws and teeth soon found their way into Hyde's flesh, spilling his blood all over the floor. Hyde felt his power swelling within him as he listened to the spirits' pleas for mercy mixed with hateful remarks toward those they once knew. Hyde's fists tightened as he expelled a large blast of his power purifying Alester's hatful magic from the spirits that surrounded him.

"Bravo," Alester said, clapping his hands. "Bravo indeed, Damian, but alas all for not. I have plenty more where those came from, and soon I'll have yours as well."

Alester pointed at Hyde, and as he did black electricity flew from his finger straight toward Hyde. Quickly he threw his arms together to try and block the attack. As Hyde did, he felt the electricity hit him; it felt as if thousands of needles were digging into his body. Hyde felt his muscles being torn into until the sound of a gunshot echoed into the air.

The electricity faded away, and as Hyde looked up, he saw Alester holding his face as his blood pooled on the floor below him. Rosey walked up next to Hyde and looked up at him as he straightened up.

"Let's finish this together," Rosey said with a determined stare.

"Yeah, let's kill this bastard," Hyde said as he pulled his tie off and threw it to the side.

"You bitch, you shot me in the face." Alester laughed as he looked up at Rosey and Hyde, pulling his eyepatch off in the process. "I'll drag both of you through Hell itself!" Alester laughed as phantom hands appeared around him and that black liquid leaked from his eye and mouth. Hyde readied himself. His markings began to glow brightly as he stared at Alester.

"This ends now, Alester," Hyde said as he aimed his hand at Alester and Rosey aimed her pistol. She began to pull the trigger as the hands rushed toward her and Alester dashed toward Hyde.

Alester's nails grew into jagged black talons as he lunged for Hyde's throat, only to get blasted back by a burst of magic from Hyde. Rosey flew into the air trying to escape the hands while still attempting to shoot Alester.

Hyde kicked Alester in the stomach before beginning his assault. Hyde's fists moved on their own, slamming into each side of Alester's head. The sound of bones cracking could be heard and Hyde didn't know if it was his hands or Alester's face. Hyde grabbed Alester's collar and went in for another punch but was stopped as a phantom hand grabbed his arm.

"ENOUGH!" Alester yelled, causing an explosion of his power, sending Hyde flying back toward the entrance. "I grow tired of this game, and my body is growing unstable." Alester aimed his hand at Hyde as dark energy swirled around it. "I hate to cut this short, Damian, but I need your soul." Alester smiled as several phantom hands shot out from his hand and rushed toward Hyde.

"NO!" Rosey yelled from the air and quickly flew down to save Hyde. As Rosey grabbed Hyde, the phantom hands grabbed her and pulled her into the air.

"ROSEY!" Hyde yelled, attempting to grab Rosey's hand. "Alester, you let her go now!" Hyde demanded as he stared at Alester.

"Ah, I had hoped that would work. Now, Damian are you willing to kill another woman?" Alester cackled while Rosey screamed in agony as the phantom hands dug their way into her being before dropping her to the ground. Hyde quickly ran over to Rosey and put his hand on her head.

"Stay with me, Rosey. Stay strong. I'm gonna fix this." Hyde panicked, trying to focus his magic as Rosey screamed and squirmed in his arms all while Alester laughed maniacally behind him.

"H-Hy-HYDE" Rosey's once-gentle voice cracked and distorted as she grabbed at Hyde's shirt, her gentle brown eyes slowly beginning to fog over.

"YES, DAMIAN! SAVE HER, JUST LIKE YOU SAVED SAMMY THAT NIGHT HA-HA-HA-HA-HA-HA-HA-HA-HA!"

Hyde held Rosey, trying to focus until he felt a stabbing pain in his side.

"Sh-shit," Hyde mumbled before getting thrown into a nearby wall.

"YOU LIED TO ME!" Rosey yelled as she stood up, her once nicely kept hair now a tangled mess that seemed to move on its own in an unnatural way. "YOU ALWAYS PUT EVERYONE BEFORE YOUR PROMISE!" Rosey screamed as she flew toward Hyde and tackled him into the wall, digging her claw-like talons into him before throwing him to the ground.

"A-ah s-shit, Ro-Rosey," Hyde said, stumbling to his feet only to be knocked to the ground again and again. Each time he saw more of his blood pour out of him.

"WHY COULDN'T YOU SAVE ME, HYDE? WHY DID YOU LIE TO ME?" Rosey threw Hyde against a wall and watched him cough up blood.

"Ro-Rosey, y-y-you ha-have to fi-fight this," Hyde said, slowly getting to his feet and leaning against the wall he was thrown into. "Th-this isn't y-you." Hyde coughed up more blood as he held the large wound in his stomach.

"Oh, but Damian, this is her. This is all of the emotion she hid from you, all of her hatred for you," Alester called out as he walked next to Rosey before pointing at Hyde. "Kill him, darling. Bring me his soul."

Hyde chuckled as he looked into Rosey's cloudy eyes, her once-beautiful face now a gaunt horror that stared into him.

"Fight this, Rosey," Hyde muttered as he weakly stepped away from the wall. Blood poured from his wounds like a gory waterfall as he limped toward Rosey.

"LIAR!" Rosey yelled as she flew toward Hyde, tackling him once again.

Rain pelted the dock as lightning split the sky and thunder roared above head. Hyde pushed through the crowd and eventually got to the front to see what was being auctioned off.

"Can I get two hundred for this beautiful Rolls-Royce Wraith?" the auctioneer called out to the crowd. "She's in perfect condition. Not one scratch on her."

"Four hundred!" Hyde called out, raising his hand and a stack of cash. "I'll take it," Hyde said as he handed the money to the man.

"Well then, sir, she's all yours." The man smiled as he handed Hyde the keys. The crowd sighed and complained as Hyde got into the car and started it.

"Well, she starts. That's good," Hyde said to himself as he drove off.

"Of course she starts, asshole," a voice said from the back seat after some time of driving, startling Hyde.

"Fuckin' Christ, lady. How'd you get in here?" Hyde said, pulling off to the side of the road.

"Well, this is my car," the lady said with a smile as she watched Hyde get out before following him.

"If it's yours, why was it at a police auction?" Hyde asked, watching the lady leave the back seat.

"Well," the lady looked down as if looking for the right words, "she was my car, but you see, I'm dead." The lady smiled and held her hand out to Hyde. "Where are my manners. Rosey Ann, and you are?"

"Hyde, paranormal investigator." Hyde smiled as he shook Rosey's hand.

"Oh, a PI for ghosts, huh." Rosey smiled as she crossed her arms. "Sounds kinda silly, don't ya think?" she asked while looking up at Hyde.

"Yeah, I used to think so, but more and more spirits keep asking me for help, and I'm not one to say no to someone in need."

"Ah, one of those hero types, huh?" Rosey laughed.

"I guess so, yeah." The rain fell harder on the two as lightning lit up the sky.

"Well, I guess we're partners now," Rosey said, walking to the passenger's side of the car.

"Partners?" Hyde asked as he opened the driver's side door.

"Well yeah, I'm not just gonna ride along with you." Rosey smiled as she watched Hyde start the car. "One condition, though."

"And that is?" Hyde asked as he pulled back onto the road.

"Help me find who killed me," Rosey said, pulling a pack of cigarettes out from under her seat.

"Deal," Hyde said, lighting Rosey's cigarette with a snap.

Hyde held Rosey as she slowly returned back to her normal form. A pool of blood had formed beneath both of them as Hyde tightened his grip around Rosey.

"H-Hyde," Rosey said as she slowly looked down only for Hyde to stop her.

"D-don't lo-look." Hyde chuckled weakly. "I'm gl-glad y-you're ba-back." Hyde coughed up blood as his knees buckled and him and Rosey knelt to the floor.

"No, no, no, no, Hyde." Rosey wrapped her free arm around Hyde as he leaned on her. "I'm sorry. I'm so sorry. Please no." Hyde grabbed Rosey's wrist and slowly pulled her hand out of his chest. As he did, blood sprayed out onto Rosey and the floor.

"Shh, I-I'm okay. I-I pr-promise." Hyde smiled weakly at Rosey as he leaned away from her.

"Hyde, I-I di-didn't mean to." Rosey's voice broke as tears fell down her face. Hyde wrapped an arm around Rosey and held her tightly.

"C-cut th-the waterw-works." Hyde chuckled as he slowly fell to the floor. "Y-you g-g-got th-this."

"No, Hyde, don't leave me. Please don't go." Rosey tried to stop the wound in Hyde's chest from bleeding. "Come on, i-it's just a-a scratch, ri-right?" Rosey's vision blurred as her tears fell faster and faster. "Right, Hyde? R-right." Rosey put her head on Hyde's chest. The heartbeat she used to love listening to wasn't there anymore, Rosey gripped Hyde's bloody shirt tightly as she sobbed into his chest uncontrollably.

"BEAUTIFUL PERFORMANCE, DARLING! TRULY SPLENDID!" Alester shouted from behind Rosey as she knelt before him.

"Please come back, Hyde." Rosey lifted her head up and gently touched Hyde's cheek. As she did, Rosey felt her anger toward Alester welling up within her. Alester's mocking only fed this feeling inside her. Rosey held Hyde's hand tightly as her hair slowly began to stand on end, and black and purple electricity sparked around her as she felt something within her snap.

"AHHHHHHHHH!" Rosey screamed loudly as she threw her head back, shattering the windows in the room and blasting Alester back, slamming him into his desk. The electricity grew more and more violent as Rosey slowly began to float into the air, carefully letting go of Hyde's hand.

Alester stood up from the wreck of his desk and looked at Rosey as she floated in the air and stared him down. He could feel the hateful power resonating within her and Alester couldn't help but smile.

"Yes, yes, yes! COME ON, ROSE! COME AND FIGHT ME!" Alester shouted out to Rosey, but she heard nothing. She felt nothing, nothing but hatred and bloodlust.

Chapter Twelve:
Banshee's Scream

Alester smiled as he stared at Rosey. Electricity sparked off her as the air around her swirled violently. Her eyes were now fog-covered pits of rage, and the feeling of her bloodlust was orgasmic to Alester.

"Yes, yes, YES!" Alester opened his arms wide, beckoning Rosey to attack him. "Let me feel your anger, just as Damian did. HIT ME WITH EVERYTHING YOU'VE GOT!" Alester laughed as Rosey quickly flew toward him, digging her claws into his body as she slammed him into a wall then the ceiling before throwing him to the ground.

Alester chuckled as he coughed up blood after hitting the ground. The sound of his ribs breaking got his heart racing and the pain of standing made him laugh maniacally as he waited for Rosey's next attack. Wind rushed through the broken windows, picking up the scattered shards of glass and broken pieces of wood that were strewn about the room.

"You're truly beautiful, my dear. A gorgeous banshee of hatred and anger." Alester held his arms out to Rosey as she slowly floated down from the air. "I haven't felt this way in a long long time." Alester chuckled as he grabbed his wounded side, black blood leaked out from within him as he cackled like the demon he was.

"You sicken me. Filth like you doesn't deserve to breathe," Rosey said before charging at Alester once again, only for him to grab her hair and slam her to the ground. The phantom hands then quickly began to tear away at her soul.

"You spirits are the real filth, disgusting shadows of humanity." Alester stomped on Rosey's head as he degraded her while she screamed in pain. "Your being pisses me off and you belong in Hell with that idiot Damian." Alester laughed until he was blasted back by Rosey.

"DON'T YOU DARE INSULT HIM, YOU MONSTER!" Rosey yelled as she turned Alester's phantom hands against him. Alester's vision blurred as blood leaked from his head; he soon felt the stabbing pain of the hands clawing into his body. Rosey floated over to Alester as bits of his body were ripped off and his black ooze-like blood sprayed into the air.

"ENOUGH!" Alester yelled, dispelling the hands and forcing Rosey into a far away wall. "I will not be beaten by some bitch ghost who thinks they can use my powers against me." Alester stood up as dark shadows swirled around him, slowly repairing his body; the sound of his bones snapping back into place sounded off in the midst of the chaotic room. Alester chuckled as he regained his composure and cracked his neck. "Ahh, much better," Alester said as he locked eyes with Rosey.

Rosey chuckled as she floated into the air, licking the black blood off her claws with her long snake-like tongue. Alester clapped his hands as he looked Rosey up and down before suddenly teleporting in front of her and forcing his knee into her stomach.

"You only have this power because of me. Remember that, girl." Alester went to move away, but Rosey dug her claws into his leg before he could and slammed him into the wall behind her.

"How's it feel to die by your own power then, bastard?" Rosey laughed as she watched Alester's body fade away into a cloud of black smoke. "Coward, quit running and face me!" Rosey demanded as she looked around the room. As she did, she saw Alester reappear in the center of the room.

"You're going to witness true power, something that can only be found in the deepest pits of Hell itself." Alester knelt to the ground as the symbol he stood upon began to glow dark crimson. "Once I have this power, I'll become truly IMMORTAL!"

"YOU'RE INSANE!" Rosey yelled as she dashed toward Alester in hopes to pull him out of the symbol, but as she got closer she was blasted back as a hoard of damned spirits flew toward Alester.

"Insanity is the price one must pay in order to achieve true power." Alester smiled as the spirits flew into his body, causing it to spaz around and bend unnaturally. Alester choked as the torchered souls forced themselves down his throat; his fingers bent and broke as sharp claws tore through his flesh. Rosey stepped back as she watched Alester's body get torn apart from the inside out as something inhuman attempted to crawl out of him.

Alester coughed up blood as a long boney arm clawed out of his mouth. His jaw snapped and his neck cracked as faces pushed out from under his skin. Large black horns ripped out from his forehead as his body began to float up into the air.

"Y-Yes, it feels so good to be flesh again," a hellish voice exclaimed from within Alester's body as it dropped to the ground.

Rosey stepped back, her body slowly fading back to her original form as her knees grew weak.

"I-I can't." Rosey dropped to her knees as Alester left the symbol. The air around him grew heavy, the sounds of hundreds of tortured souls screamed out for mercy from within him as he walked toward Rosey. "Hy-Hyde, please h-help me," Rosey said as tears welled up behind her eyes.

"Do not cry, child. Soon you will be with him again," Alester said as he picked Rosey up by her hair. Rosey felt her very being beginning to get pulled into Alester's body until suddenly an explosion of magic erupted between them, sending both Alester and Rosey flying back.

Rosey looked up as after she recovered, and for a brief moment saw Hyde standing between her and Alester. Rosey weakly reached out to Hyde as he faded away, but not before giving her a thumbs up.

"H-Hyde." Rosey's hand tightened into a fist as she slowly stood up, her nails sharpened once again. "I don't care how much power you have. I don't care what you think you are. Because to me," Rosey floated into the air as a mix of purple and black electricity sparked around her fingers, "you're nothing but a waste of air."

"Tough talk for someone who's on their way to hell!" Alester shouted as he cracked his neck. "Your soul is mine bitch!" Alester said, pointing at Rosey.

"Come get it, bastard," Rosey demanded as she quickly flew toward Alester, slashing at him with her claws and dodging his counters, flying out of his reach only to dive back at him like a hunger predator going in for the kill.

Alester chuckled as he and Rosey flew into the air and began to pumble one another. Each took turns slamming the other into the walls and ceiling. Even though Rosey wanted to give up and die again, she felt determined to avenge everyone Alester had killed, and she wasn't going to let Hyde down.

Rosey tackled Alester and threw him to the ground, causing the floor to crack and break apart under him. Without giving him time to recover, Rosey aimed her hands at him and watched as the electricity that sparked around her hands quickly flew down and hit Alester.

The sound of his screams echoed out into the room as Rosey focused on putting everything she could into her attack before quickly flying down and forcing her fist into Alester's monstrous face.

"DIE, DIE, DIE, DIE, YOU MONSTER!" Rosey screamed as she punched Alester over and over again. She couldn't stop herself; it was as if her arms were moving on their own.

"Enough!" Alester exclaimed as he grabbed Rosey by the throat and threw her away from him as he stood up. "I grow tired of this game we're playing. Accept your fate and join us." Alester pointed a clawed finger at Rosey as she stood up.

"I'd rather suffer in Hell than join you!" Rosey shouted back.

"Then suffer." Alester opened his hand and watched as a dark red beam fired from his hand and quickly closed in on Rosey.

Rosey wanted to move; she wanted to do anything but stand there. However, her legs felt numb and she didn't have the strength to fight anymore. Visions of what Hell might be filled her mind until she felt a firm hand grab her shoulder, snapping her out of her trance. Rosey took a deep breath as her body moved on her own.

The sound of an explosion sounded off through the room quieting the chaos that was once storming through it. Alester laughed as he looked at the hole where Rosey once was.

"I hope Hell is warm eno—" Alester stopped and looked down at his arm. "Wait, where the hell is my—"

"Arm?" Rosey cut Alester off as he turned around to see her holding his disembodied arm, black blood still pouring out from it.

"You bitch, give tha—" Alester was cut off as Rosey kicked him in the side of his head, causing it to spin completely around.

"Shut the hell up and die, prick," Rosey said as she stabbed her hand into Alester's chest before slashing his throat with her other hand. She watched as Alester fell to his knees and grabbed his throat.

"I am Alester, son of Lucifer. I will not die to you!" Alester's voice was muffled as blood filled his mouth until Rosey kicked his head one last time, sending it flying away from his body. His body fell to the ground and the spirits within him began to fly away slowly fading as they reached the sky. Rosey smiled as the screams were replaced with gratitude and smiles.

"Hyde!" Rosey exclaimed as she quickly ran over toward Hyde's body. "Hey, we did it," Rosey said as she knelt down and gently lifted Hyde onto her lap. "H-Hyde, wake up. We d-did it." Tears slowly fell down Rosey's cheeks as she held Hyde's body.

"Cut the waterworks, Rosey."

Rosey looked behind her and saw Hyde standing there smiling.

"H-Hyde?" Rosey smiled as she quickly ran toward Hyde and wrapped her arms around him. "I'm so sorry! I-I didn't—"

"Hey, it's okay." Hyde cut Rosey's apology off as he held her. "Look, I ain't got much time, Rose," Hyde said as he stepped back and showed her a chain that had wrapped itself around his wrist.

"N-no, you can't leave. I-I need you here. I have so much left to say." Rosey looked up at Hyde as he stared at the sunrise through the broken windows.

"Ya know, I never thought I'd die in this city." Hyde chuckled as he turned to face Rosey. "Thank you, Rose, for everything." Hyde put a hand on Rosey's head and messed with her hair. "You made life just that much more interesting." Hyde smiled as he looked down at Rosey. She hadn't seen that smile in so long she had forgotten how sweet it looked.

"Please stay," Rosey said, grabbing Hyde's hand gently as he pulled it off her head.

"Bye, Rose." Hyde hugged Rosey one last time before slowly fading away. As he did, the door opened and Lynn rushed inside to see the destroyed room and Rosey standing among the chaos, staring at the sunrise through the broken windows.

"Rosey?" Lynn slowly walked up to Rosey as she wiped her tears away. "Where's Hyde?" Lynn asked as she looked around.

"H-he, um, he died." Rosey covered her face as she sobbed into her hands. Lynn put a hand on her shoulder before pulling Rosey into a hug.

"I'm so sorry, Rosey." Lynn let go of Rosey as she pushed away gently.

"Cut the waterworks. That's what he'd say right now." Rosey chuckled as she walked past Lynn.

Days had passed since Rosey killed Alester. She and Lynn decided to have a small funeral for Hyde and Alan as a way to fully put their spirits to rest. The two of them now spent most of their time at the AfterLife drinking and remembering. Tonight was no different for Rosey. She was enjoying a somewhat decent White Russian when she felt a tap on her shoulder.

"Excuse me, miss,. but you wouldn't happen to be Rosey, the paranormal investigator, would you?" a woman said softly as Rosey turned around.

"Yeah, why? You got a problem with something spooky?" Rosey said with a smile.

www.ingramcontent.com/pod-product-compliance
Lightning Source LLC
Chambersburg PA
CBHW052049150726
48002CB00002B/814